STEVEN GRAY

YUMA BREAK-OUT

Complete and Unabridged

LINFORD
Leicester

First published in Great Britain in 1999 by
Robert Hale Limited
London

First Linford Edition
published 2000
by arrangement with
Robert Hale Limited
London

British Library CIP Data

Gray, Steven
    Yuma break-out.—Large print ed.—
Linford western library
    1. Western stories
    2. Large type books
    I. Title
    823.9'14 [F]

    ISBN 0–7089–5631–9

Published by
F. A. Thorpe (Publishing) Ltd.
Anstey, Leicestershire

Set by Words & Graphics Ltd.
Anstey, Leicestershire
Printed and bound in Great Britain by
T. J. International Ltd., Padstow, Cornwall

1

Trouble started over the slop called breakfast.

Ted Hayes was in line behind a bully who went by the nickname of 'Growler'. Growler was an extremely large man with greasy hair, few teeth and a broken nose. Five years earlier he'd been sent to Yuma for manslaughter and, because of his size and temperament, liked to think of himself as the most feared person in the prison; which he had been until Hayes's arrival. He felt Hayes challenged him for the position of top dog and didn't like it. Was always looking for ways to do Hayes down.

'Hey,' he now growled. 'You've got more'n me.'

Hayes looked down at both their plates, thinking it would hardly matter as the food was practically uneatable anyway. 'No, I ain't.'

His heart began to pound, knowing Growler was about to start something, getting ready to deal with the man. He'd never looked to take over Growler's position. Never sought to mess with the man. At the same time he'd never backed down from facing up to him. Such a display of cowardice was not in Hayes's nature. He also knew that to give in to Growler would not mean being left alone while the man enjoyed his triumph, but being mercilessly taunted by him. No way was that going to happen.

So now when Growler said, 'Yeah, you have,' and pushed Hayes in the chest, Hayes didn't hesitate.

He said, 'Well you have goddamned all of it then.' And tipped the contents of his plate over Growler's head.

Several of the men round them giggled, which didn't improve Growler's mood.

'You bastard!' he yelled, clawing the mess out of his eyes. 'I'll have you for that.' His hands reached out to grab at the other man but, with a contemptuous sneer, Hayes moved quickly out of the way. Growler was left to clean himself up as best as he could.

'See that?' Harvey Murdoch said to Rob Cameron. The two men had already got their breakfast and were sitting eating it at a far table. 'Ted's goin' to be in trouble again if he ain't careful.'

Cameron nodded, worried. He cast an anxious glance around. Luckily none of the guards had witnessed the exchange; they wouldn't have let it pass if they had. But this time the problem didn't lie with them. Growler was hardly likely to forget or forgive what had happened. And there was little Rob could do to help. The guards made sure he and Hayes were kept apart.

★ ★ ★

It was obvious to Don Hopkins, Yuma's chief guard, that trouble was brewing.

He could feel the tension in the air. He wondered whether or not he should warn Warden Bright. But Bright didn't like to listen to problems, he only liked to hear the solutions. And Hopkins was sure he could handle whatever happened.

He bet it had something to do with Ted Hayes, and he grinned, looking forward to dealing with the man. Again. Since Hayes's arrival at Yuma, he had been a thorn in the sides of the guards and Hopkins not only wanted him broken, he wanted the pleasure of breaking him personally.

Hayes had just turned thirty. He had long stringy black hair and had lost his left eye in a knife fight. When he wanted to frighten someone he took off the black patch he normally wore to reveal the pink, scarred and empty eye socket underneath. From the first day he'd arrived he walked around Yuma like he owned it. Well, he wouldn't be the first convict to come to Yuma believing he was stronger than the system. He wouldn't be the first to find out how wrong he was.

Hopkins warned the other guards to be prepared. They were.

* * *

Trouble found Hayes in the exercise yard. Sensing something was going to happen, and soon, he was trying to avoid it by keeping out of the way. It didn't help. Growler sought him out.

Hayes saw him striding across the yard, several of those who hung about him following behind. Word quickly spread amongst the other convicts that the two enemies were going to battle it out. Hayes didn't want a fight, at the same time he wasn't about to apologise. He straightened. Which was all he had time for.

Yelling, 'You bastard,' Growler rushed him.

The man hit Hayes full on and they went down on the dusty ground, grabbing and kicking.

With cries of encouragement and excitement, the convicts crowded round. They didn't really mind which one of the men won; they just wanted to see blood.

'Hell,' Cameron said, trying to push his way to the front.

'There ain't nothin' you can do,' Murdoch warned, pulling Cameron back. 'You interfere, you'll have Growler's friends to answer to. Or worse. Ted can handle himself.'

Normally, yes. But Cameron saw that from somewhere Growler had got hold of a weapon. He called out, 'Look out, Ted, he's got a knife.'

Hayes didn't waste time worrying about where Growler had found a weapon. Instantly he grabbed the man's hand, holding the knife away from him, while trying to get out from under the man.

Coming up hard against the wall, seeing nothing but the legs of other men, Hayes found himself being pulled to his feet. Growler's knee smashed into his stomach and Hayes doubled over, gasping for breath. Somehow he managed to retain a hold on Growler's knife hand. Hayes was slammed back against the wall. The knife came closer to his remaining eye, while Growler's ugly face broke into a laugh. The man wanted to blind him!

With a surge of anger, Hayes used all his strength to knock Growler's hand away and the knife span to the ground. It was quickly picked up and pocketed by another prisoner.

Yelling in outrage, Growler caught Hayes round the waist, squeezing hard, trying to break his back.

Kicking his opponent's knee, making Growler squeal in pain, Hayes wrenched his arms free. He was in a killing mood. No longer cared about the consequences. As hard as he could he clapped both hands against Growler's ears. Momentarily stunned, the man stumbled backwards. Hayes hit him, breaking his already broken nose, then punched him in the mouth. Growler would have fallen if he were not being held up by some of his friends.

Hayes dodged away, fists up and ready, prepared to inflict more serious damage. To end this once and for all.

No doubt he now had the upper hand. Would have won. Perhaps killed Growler. It was then that Hopkins decided the fun had lasted long enough, and the guards intervened.

'Outta the way!' Hopkins yelled. And he and five or six guards bullied their way through the mess of prisoners, striking out with gun barrels, fists and boots.

They reached the two men just as they were about to fling themselves at one another again. Growler was pushed aside and jumped on by a couple of the guards, while Hopkins and the remaining three men turned their attention on Hayes. Hopkins swung his rifle viciously. The end caught Hayes in the ribs and with a little cry he went down on the ground. Immediately the four men circled him, kicking violently, grunting with the effort, eyes alight with pleasure.

'Oh God,' Cameron moaned. He would have tried to stop them had not Murdoch stopped him. He turned angrily to the other man. 'They'll kill him!'

'No they won't. Hopkins don't want that. He wants Ted alive and eating outta his damned hand.'

Cameron turned away, unwilling to watch the punishment inflicted on his friend.

Hayes lay, trying to make himself as small as possible to avoid the boots smashing into his body. He groaned, almost passing out.

At last Hopkins said, 'Leave him be.'

Hands dragged Hayes up, and he hung head down, supported by two guards. He felt nothing but pain, saw nothing but blackness.

Hopkins stepped in front of him. 'Think yourself lucky, boy. I'm in a good mood today. If I weren't, it'd be the hole for you. As it is, you can spend some time all alone — chained up in your cell, considering your sins.' The man looked up at the cloudless sky and smiled. 'I reckon it'll be almost as hot in there as in the hole anyway. Go on, take the stupid sonofabitch away.'

Hayes was dragged away, biting on his already swollen lips in an effort not to give his tormentors the satisfaction of hearing him moan. Cameron spoke to him as he went by but the guards roughly pushed him out of the way, and Hayes had no idea what he said.

Hopkins turned to the few remaining convicts. 'Fun's over! Get on with whatever you should be doing. Hurry it up.'

Hayes was pushed into his cell and chained to the floor. He lay helpless, the sun beating down on him, the temperature soaring in the confined space. Every part of his body ached. He feared his ribs were broken. He felt sick, kept losing consciousness. His good eye was almost closed and several teeth were loosened. Yet he could almost smile. He wasn't broken yet. And never would be.

2

'Come on, move it.'

As Ted Hayes emerged from the tiny, stifling cell, he took little notice of the guard. Instead he blinked his one brown eye up at the sky. It was cloudless, a brilliant blue even this early in the morning. Already hot.

Ever eager to impose more hurt, the guard shoved the barrel of his rifle into Hayes's back, sniggering as Hayes stumbled. The guard was fat, with a lard-like belly, and it was going to give Hayes tremendous pleasure to slit the bastard's throat.

Because Hayes was making plans.

He didn't intend to spend another summer, with its over-powering heat, in the hellhole that was the Arizona Territorial Prison at Yuma. He, Rob Cameron and Harvey Murdoch had already served two years there, and that was two years too long.

'What you grinning about, boy?' the guard snarled.

'Nothin',' Hayes muttered in reply.

'I hope not. I wouldn't like to think you was funning me.'

Hardly recovered from his last beating — after several days this was the first time he'd been freed from the chains in his cell — Hayes didn't want another one. So he dared do nothing but give the guard a sulky glare of insolence. Bunching his hands into fists, the guard's laughter following him, he walked away from the cells to the yard where the prisoners were allowed to exercise.

No one came near him. Not just because of his uncertain temper and angry disposition, but also because he was always in trouble with the guards. The other men were afraid to be seen with him for fear of being tarred with the same brush.

He didn't mind being on his own. It had always been like that and he was used to it. He'd only ever had one friend, either inside or out of prison, and that was Rob Cameron. They'd known each other for a long time. Understood one another.

When he reached the yard he quickly spotted Cameron, who was lounging over by the far wall. Being members of the same gang, convicted at the same time for the same crime, they weren't meant to associate with one another. However, they had soon worked out that by walking around the yard in opposite directions they could, in passing, carry on a conversation. Now seeing all the guards were busy and not taking a great deal of notice of what was going on, Hayes took the chance to wander over to join his friend. With luck, they could get a few minutes undisturbed talk.

Cameron saw him coming and smiled in relief, even though Hayes looked like hell. 'You OK?'

'I've felt better.'

'I bet. The bastards.'

'How's Growler?'

'He was put in the hole. We ain't seen him since.'

'Good. Perhaps the sonofabitch is dead. Save me killing him.'

Cameron steered the talk away from a revenge Hayes would probably never have the chance of carrying out. 'You thought any more about gettin' away? It ain't gonna be easy.' His hands thrust in his trouser pockets, he added, 'We could get ourselves shot.'

He sounded worried. While Hayes sometimes took notice of what he said, most times no one could reason Ted out of what he'd made up his mind to do. From past experience, he could see Hayes was ready to explode. He didn't want Hayes to act first and think later, and perhaps get into more unnecessary trouble.

Cameron was twenty-seven. Tall and slender, he had fair hair, blue eyes and an innocent expression that had fooled a number of unfortunate people. He'd met Hayes ten years ago when he was working as a cowhand on a small ranch in East Texas. Hayes had ridden by and immediately appeared to the hard working youngster to be a dashing figure with no cares in the world.

They had gone to a nearby saloon and hung out for a while, Cameron listening to every word of Hayes's exaggerated stories of his exploits. Easily influenced, Cameron had helped Hayes to rob his employer, and then ridden off with him.

Except that they'd ended up in Yuma, he'd never regretted taking up a life of crime and violence.

'It'd be better to get shot than stay here another twenty-three years.' Already Hayes was covered with sweat, hardly able to breathe. 'I doubt I could stand that.'

'What you got in mind?'

'Been working on somethin'.' Actually, Hayes had no idea how they could get away. He just knew they had to. 'Have you spoken to Harve about it?'

'Yeah.'

16

'What does he say?'

'He'll go along with whatever you decide.'

Hayes wasn't surprised. Harvey Murdoch was the oldest member of the gang. He was only a thief because he liked to earn his money without working for it, and had been in jail several times. He spent his time gambling and carefully keeping out of trouble, and was too lazy and too scared of Hayes to resist anything he suggested. Because Murdoch was a member of the gang, Hayes would try to look out for him; but he was someone who was ultimately expendable. Just like other gang members in the past.

'I think —'

'Hey, you two, no talking!' A guard yelled. 'Break it up, or I'll come over there and break you both.'

'Best go, see you later,' Cameron said.

Dispirited, Hayes walked away.

Yuma!

Yuma — hated, feared. Nothing Hayes had heard about the place could have prepared him for the reality.

Situated on the banks of the Colorado River where it joined the Gila, the prison stood in the middle of a pitiless desert. Escape seemed almost impossible, for it was surrounded by eighteen-foot-high adobe walls with a guard tower at each corner, and a gate tower equipped with a gatling-gun. And the guards patrolled day and night.

The cells were nine foot square and exposed to the sun. In them, the convicts were chained to the stone floors all night. During the long summer months, the heat made it almost impossible to sleep. The food was bad, the water warm and foul.

Even worse, the days were boring, full of brutality. Hard labour on the chain-gang was perhaps no worse than sitting round for hours with nothing to do. Overseen by guards who, as bored and brutal as the prisoners, took every opportunity to inflict punishment, the convicts suffered physically and mentally.

And known as a trouble-maker, Hayes suffered more than most. The guards, encouraged by Warden Bright and Chief Hopkins, were out to discipline him any chance that came their way. He'd been whipped, spent days in solitary confinement in a pitch-black cell, and been shut without water in the hole in the ground, where he thought he'd go mad.

Now he didn't intend to suffer any more.

Surely with only twenty guards to look after some two hundred and eighty convicts, there must be a way to overpower them. If some of the prisoners got killed too, tough. He didn't care about them, so long as he and Rob, and Murdoch, escaped.

If anyone had bothered to notice they would have seen a peculiar glint in Hayes's one eye, a glint that spelled trouble for anyone who tried to stop him.

And when he did escape, the first thing he was going to do was go after Glen Kramer — damn the traitorous sonofabitch to hell and back!

3

'Here you are, sweetheart, coffee,' Leonie said, coming up to where her husband was carefully weeding a long line of vegetables.

Glen Kramer straightened up and stretched, easing the kinks out of his back. He took the cup from Leonie's hand. 'Thanks.'

'Are you nearly finished?' Leonie asked.

'There's just a little bit more to do.'

Together they surveyed Glen's work and smiled at one another, well satisfied. Cucumbers, canteloupes, beans and tomatoes all grew in orderly, well irrigated lines down to the river's edge.

'You're going to have a lot of vegetables to take in to Mr MacKenzie.'

'I know. I hope he'll be pleased.'

With luck, Mr MacKenzie would pay him enough for all this fresh produce so as well as buying the food he and Leonie couldn't grow themselves, Glen could put some money towards the seed-drill he wanted; and perhaps buy Leonie a present.

'How soon do you think you'll be able to go into town?'

'Couple of days time, probably.' For a moment Glen looked worried. 'You know I'll be gone nearly all day. I'll have to start early and won't get back till late afternoon.'

'We've already talked about that. You've got to go. Mr MacKenzie won't come out here.'

'Are you sure you'll be all right on your own?'

'Of course I will.'

'You can come with me if you like.'

'No. There's plenty to do here. The ground needs hoeing and those seedlings near the house want watering every day. And there are the animals to see to as well.'

'Can you manage all that by yourself?'

Leonie's green eyes flashed indignantly. 'I grew up on a farm, remember?'

Glen grinned, enjoying teasing her. Leonie was slender, and only came up to his shoulder, but despite her delicate looks she was well able to pull her weight. Not only in the house but on the farm as well. He put an arm round her waist, ignoring her squeal of protest at his dirty hands, and kissed her.

'Stop it! I'm too busy and so are you. And dinner's nearly ready. Beef, beans and homemade biscuits. You must be starving.'

'I'll be there,' Glen kissed her again. Leonie pulled away, and he watched as she walked up the slope to the farmhouse. Her copper coloured hair seemed to blaze in the afternoon light, making his heart beat faster.

Then he turned back to completing his work for the day.

Buying this farm had to be the second best thing he'd ever done in his life. Though only a short time ago, if anyone had told him he'd make a hard working farmer he would have laughed at them.

It was good land, situated alongside the river and rising gently into cypress-covered hills. And the place was already thriving. As well as vegetables they had several chickens and a milk cow.

The farmhouse was sturdy, and as it was made of adobe it was cool in summer, warm in winter. Of course it was also small, consisting of three rooms — parlour, kitchen and bedroom — and furnished only with necessities. Not perfect by any means. But Leonie always kept it clean and tidy and gathered wild flowers to display in tin cups that passed for vases. She was also a good cook.

For, of course, the very best thing he'd ever done was marry Leonie. He'd met her in Flagstaff while on the run from both the law and Ted Hayes. She'd seen something in him no one else ever had; had made him believe in himself. Even after he'd told her about his past, she'd agreed to leave her safe family life to go with him.

He still couldn't believe how, with her help, he'd turned his life around. At twenty he was an outlaw, in danger of being caught and put in jail; perhaps of being shot and killed. Two years later he was here on his own farm — well, all right, not his own yet, the bank owned the mortgage on it, but so far each and every payment had been made on time — and with a wife he loved very much.

Glen felt he couldn't ask for anything more. But while he could mostly put his past life behind him, there were times he felt he didn't deserve all this happiness, and still feared the arrival of a lawman on his doorstep to make it all go wrong.

* * *

Watched by an admiring group of seven or eight small boys, United States Marshal Jubal Judd walked

25

out into the field at the back of the livery stable for his afternoon gun practice. He set up six tin cups on the fence and walked away from them, his new badge glinting in the sunlight.

While good with a rifle, his favoured weapons were his two Colt .45s in their fancy leather holsters.

Now suddenly he span round on one foot, at the same time using his left hand to draw one of the guns. He fired, almost, it seemed, without aiming. Five of the cups span into the air. Not being so good with his left hand as his right he missed the sixth. To make up for that, while the cups were still spinning in the air, he drew his second Colt with his right hand, and to a collective 'Oooh' from the boys, shot all five tin cups again before they could fall to the ground.

As he carefully reloaded the guns, the boys rushed forward to fight over who would keep the tin cups.

'You hit all of 'em,' one boy called.

'Course I did,' Judd said, nodding his head in acknowledgement.

'Two bullets in the last cup!'

He walked back to the town, the boys skipping alongside their hero.

Judd was in his early thirties and, newly promoted, was one of the youngest US marshals operating in the West.

For the moment he was sharing an office with the town marshal, and as he went inside the man looked up and said, 'Hot out there, ain't it?'

'Sure is.' Judd took off his hat and ran a hand through his hair. He glanced into the scrap of glass serving as a mirror, to make sure he was clean and tidy.

Over six feet tall, his fair hair hung in curls almost to his shoulders. He had light brown eyes and a neatly trimmed, fair moustache. He always wore black suits and white shirts, the only spot of colour being his richly decorated vests. The one he had on just now was dark blue with light blue leaves entwined over it.

With his polished boots and small feather stuck in the hatband of his Stetson, there were some who called him a dandy, but somehow they never dared say it to his face.

'Heard anything about what your first job is likely to be?'

'Not yet.'

The town marshal hid a sigh, hoping Judd's assignment would come through soon. For the younger man, with his overweening sense of his own consequence, was not an easy companion, especially for someone who hoped for an easy life.

Judd was also anxious for something important to do. He wanted the responsibility of making his own decisions, not simply following someone else's orders.

He was ambitious, anxious to do well, and didn't intend to sit in an office letting the deputy marshals claim all the glory to be found in the territory of Arizona. And he didn't want other people, jealous of him, forgetting about his past successes, saying he wasn't up to the job and that his promotion was due simply to political connections and influence.

4

Warden Bright stood at the window of his office, looking out at the guards arranging the day's work details. To anyone who knew him, especially if he came from amongst the convicts. 'Bright' was a singularly inappropriate name for the plump, vicious and dour prison warden.

Behind the gloomy face was a sharp mind, always on the lookout for ways of making money. He had requested the position at Yuma not just because it was the sort of place where he could indulge his sadistic nature, but also because it seemed to him he could make a profit there. So far he hadn't been disappointed with either aspect. The only drawback was it meant having to be in close proximity to convicts, whom he considered the scum of the earth.

A knock on the door heralded the

entrance of Chief Guard Hopkins.

'What is it?' Bright turned from the window.

'Sir!' Hopkins saluted. 'We're two short to send out on the chain-gang. Several of the convicts are sick, or — '

Bright waved an impatient hand. He didn't want to hear excuses. He wanted results. Especially when he'd already accepted bribes and pay-offs for the work the convicts were currently doing.

'Sort it out. That's what I pay you for.'

'Yes, sir.' Perhaps the only person at Yuma not scared of Bright, Hopkins stood his ground. He didn't intend to take more decisions than he had to, in case anything went wrong. 'I could put Hayes on it, but Cameron and Murdoch are already going out. And you gave orders that the three of them should be kept well apart.'

'Is he well enough?'

Hopkins shrugged. 'He's recovered.'

Stroking his chin, Bright looked out of the window again. Ted Hayes.

Someone who had to be watched all the time. Not yet cowed, despite the guards' best efforts. The other two following him. Yet what could Hayes do, either alone or with his companions, chained and guarded on the work detail? And whatever else he was, Hayes wasn't a slacker, he worked as hard as anyone. The job was already behind schedule. It wouldn't do to let it get any further behind. It was worth taking the chance.

'Put him on it as well,' he ordered. 'And, Hopkins, you go along with them. Keep an eye on the situation.'

★ ★ ★

Led by the wagon containing two water barrels, the guards riding on either side, the convicts were marched out of the prison gates. Or rather, given their shackles, they shambled.

Shuffling along at the head of the line, Hayes was surprised to see Cameron and Murdoch some way behind him. Warden Bright had given orders all three should never go out at the same time. Perhaps, with them altogether outside of the prison, this would be a good opportunity for escape.

Some hope, Hayes thought with a grimace. Not only were they wearing ankle chains that restricted movement, but for the journey to and from the work site they were also chained together in one long line. And they were accompanied by five well-armed guards, who wouldn't hesitate to shoot.

'Hell, hot, ain't it?' Miller, a young black man, muttered from behind Hayes.

'Sure is.'

'No talking! Hurry it up! We ain't got all day!' That was Hopkins. It was unusual for him to do something so lowly as accompanying the chain-gang, and he didn't look too happy about it.

Deliberate slackers felt the touch of the guards' boots or rifle butts, as they were chivvied the five miles to where the work was going on.

Hayes felt it wouldn't be quite so bad if they were actually doing something worthwhile. But they were building a section of new road coming from nowhere, and, as far as he could see, going nowhere either. It was useless and debilitating. The only reason for it was that someone somewhere was making money out of it — at the convicts' expense.

Once they reached the halt, the chains securing the men together were released, although their ankle chains were left in place. And they were allowed a sip of water before being handed out pickaxes.

By the wagon, Cameron managed a quick, hopeful word with Hayes. 'Today?'

After that, Hopkins made sure the three of them were well separated. Hayes at one end of the line, Cameron in the middle and Murdoch at the far end.

'You know what you gotta do,'

Hopkins yelled. 'So get on with it. Let's break some ground!'

Which was easier said than done. Starved of rain, the earth was rock hard. It seemed more likely to break the pickaxes rather than the other way round.

Bathed in constant sweat, body still bruised and battered, Hayes soon ached all over. His head thumped with the heat, effort and lack of food and water.

'Look at them hills,' Miller said. 'Wouldn't it be good to be up there, where it's cool?'

Hayes turned his eyes longingly towards the foothills that were nothing but a distant smudge on the horizon. Even from here he thought he could see the green of trees indicating water; or maybe it was just his imagination. Escape! But how to escape without getting shot? He should be able to come up with something, but it was difficult when his brains were being fried in the sun and his mouth was so parched all he could think of was a long drink of cold water.

He was aware of Murdoch getting on with the work, but actually doing as little as possible, and of Cameron glancing at him once or twice, obviously wondering if this was part of his plan. If only it was. But Cameron was doomed to disappointment. Tonight would find them back at the prison.

Hayes had reckoned without Miller.

Round about noon, the guards, who suffered from the heat almost as much as the prisoners, were perhaps not as alert as they might have been. Usually by now they had allowed the convicts to stop for a while but because Hopkins was along they were following the rules set out by Warden Bright — work the men as hard as possible, with only one halt during the day. The tempers of everyone — guards and convicts alike — were at boiling point.

Suddenly Miller called out to Hopkins. 'Hey you! When the hell we gonna get a rest and somethin' to drink? It's hot, if you ain't noticed.'

'You'll go on as long as I say.'

'Oh yeah?' With a snarl, Miller flung his pickaxe to the ground.

At once Hopkins rushed up and whacked Miller round the side of the head with his rifle. Miller staggered but didn't fall. 'Pick it up, you bastard! Get back to work.'

'Like hell.'

Hopkins raised his rifle again, pleasure in his eyes.

Before the blow could fall, Miller dived forward. He grabbed hold of the axe and swung it upwards with all his might. The point was buried deep and viciously in Hopkins' chest. Eyes popping, the man collapsed on his knees, clutching at the handle. Gurgling with fright and pain, his mouth filling with blood, he fell to the sand, kicked his legs in the air and died.

Things happened quickly after that.

Another guard immediately shot

Miller, sending him sprawling backwards, arms and legs outflung, blood spurting from the wound.

The nearest convicts leapt on the guard, beating him with fists, feet and chains. A third guard jumped up onto the water wagon, spraying the men with bullets. Shots, yells and shrieks filled the hot noon air.

Hayes fell to the ground by Miller's body, thinking that was probably the safest place to avoid any stray bullets. He yelled across at Cameron, 'Get the keys!' He pointed at the shot guard, who had the bunch of keys that would free their ankle chains hanging from his waist. 'Quick!'

Amidst all the confusion, Cameron, on his knees, scrambled over to the dead guard. He yanked the keys free and flung them at Hayes, whilst gathering up the guard's rifle and revolver.

Shoving Miller's body aside, Hayes sat on the ground and reached for the lock securing the chain round his ankles. He shook so much with fear and excitement it took him several attempts — and then suddenly he was free!

He hurried up to Cameron, who was shooting at another guard and crouching down by his friend quickly unlocked his chains. 'Where's Harve?'

'Over there.'

Ever cautious Murdoch had managed to hide in the shelter of the water wagon.

And glancing that way, Hayes suddenly realized that the guard shooting from the wagon bed was his fat and flabby tormentor. Grinning, he snatched the rifle from Cameron and stood up. He levered several shots in the man's direction. And watched in satisfaction as the guard flung up his arms and tumbled back off the wagon.

'That's one bastard who won't hurt anyone else!'

Hopkins was dead too. This just had to be Hayes's day!

'Let's get Harve and get outta here.'

As Murdoch freed himself, Hayes looked round, taking in the situation. Three guards were dead, the other two still making a fight of it. Standing back to back, they kept up a continuous and effective fire. Several convicts were dead, more were wounded, while the rest were intent on killing the hated guards. None had yet thought to make their escape.

'Here.' Hayes snatched the keys from Murdoch, handing them to another convict. 'Free yourself. Get away while you can.' He didn't really care what happened to any of the others, they'd never been friends of his, but it would add to the confusion, help with their own escape.

Horses! They had to have horses.

That might not be so easy. One of the mules pulling the wagon was shot and down, the other twisted up in the harness. The two remaining guards were standing in front of three horses. No hope there. The fourth horse had skittered away.

But Hopkins's animal was near by, on the far side of the wagon. Well, one horse was better than none. And hanging from the saddle-pommel was a canteen of water. Maybe there would be more ammunition, perhaps some food, in the saddlebags.

'Come on,' Cameron urged. 'Let's go.'

'I'm goin' for the horse. You two make a start.'

'Where to?' Murdoch asked.

Hayes pointed. 'The foothills.'

As the other two dashed away from the wagon, Hayes ran, in a crouch, towards the horse. Several bullets kicked up dust near his feet. It didn't matter. They all missed.

Kicking aside another convict who had the same idea, Hayes grabbed the horse's reins. Yelling in outrage, the man caught at his arm and Hayes swung round. It was Growler!

'The horse is mine, you bastard!' Growler shouted.

'No it ain't — but this is for you.'

And Hayes fired the rifle into the man's chest.

No one was going to stop him — neither guard nor fellow prisoner, especially Growler. He vaulted up into the saddle and, digging heels into the horse's sides, sent it into a gallop, letting out a yell of triumph as he rode away.

He soon caught up with Cameron and Murdoch, and all three came to a halt, grinning at one another, teeth white in their dusty faces.

The noise and dust of the shooting and fighting was well behind them; nothing more than a cloud rising up into the still air.

There was no pursuit. How could there be? The two guards were fighting for their lives, not bothering about escaped prisoners.

They were free! They were safe!

For a while anyway.

Hayes took a drink from the canteen and passed it onto Cameron.

'What now?' Murdoch said, hands on

his knees as he leant forward, getting his breath back.

'We need different clothes from these, food and a couple more horses,' Hayes said, wiping the back of his mouth. 'And then — why, then — we find Glen Kramer.'

5

'Warden! Warden! You'd better come quick! Something's wrong!'

Now what? Didn't people know he was busy? Cursing silently, Bright heaved his body out of the chair and left his office. In the yard he was hit by the afternoon heat. 'What is it?'

'Come and see, sir.'

'This had better be good,' Bright muttered as he climbed to the top of the guard tower, sweat breaking out on his neck. He wrinkled his eyes against the glare of the sun and stared out at the desert.

Jesus! Two men — two guards — riding their horses hard for the prison!

Where were the rest of the guards? Where were the prisoners? What had happened?

'Get on down there,' he barked. 'Let

them in.' He followed slowly, his mind full of dreadful possibilities over what this meant, fearing it could mean only one thing.

By the time he reached the gates, the two riders had arrived. Their horses were lathered up, they were covered in dust and they looked scared. Most of the other guards and some of the convicts were gathered round and amidst the excited talk, Bright heard those awful words: 'Escaped . . . shooting . . . dead!'

'In my office, now!'

★   ★   ★

'Did you mean it?' Murdoch asked, wiping sweaty hands over his balding brown hair.

'Did I mean what?'

'That we were goin' after Glen Kramer.'

'Hell yes! The sonofabitch!'

The three men had come to a halt amongst a stand of rocks and juniper

45

bushes, which provided shade of sorts. It was a couple of hours since their escape, and Hayes didn't want to stop for too long.

With luck, all the guards would have been killed, and it would be some time before Warden Bright learned of what had happened. But once he did, he would immediately send men out after all the escaped convicts.

But they were hot and exhausted; they needed to rest. More importantly, so did the horse.

'Don't you want revenge on the bastard?'

'Not particularly.'

'But he got away with everything while we got put in Yuma.'

'Yeah, Ted, and we've only just got free of the place. I for one don't wanna go back, especially with what Bright'll do to us. Wouldn't it be better to go to Mexico, where we'll be safe? The border ain't far. Get some good horses, we can soon be there.'

'Hell, Mexico will still be there after

we've dealt with the kid.'

'What d'you say, Rob?'

Cameron shrugged. 'I ain't anxious to hang around here, but I don't see why the little bastard should get away with what he did.'

Murdoch sighed. He might have known Cameron would agree with Hayes. He always did.

Cameron went on, 'Think, Harve. The kid's free and clear, enjoying all the money we stole. Don't seem fair or right to me.'

'It won't do us much good if we're recaptured.'

'You can go off on your own,' Hayes suggested.

But that didn't seem right or fair to Murdoch either, because it would mean he wouldn't get the share of the spoils he'd risked as much as them to steal.

'No, I'll go with you.'

'Good, be best all round if we stick together.'

'But Ted, how do you know where to find him? He ain't likely to have stayed around Tucson. He could be anywhere by now.'

Hayes grinned. 'Oh, I think there's someone who'll tell us what we wanna know.'

'Nita, you mean?' Cameron asked.

'Yeah. Nita.'

★ ★ ★

Warden Bright bashed his hand down on the desk so hard everything on its top bounced. He couldn't believe what he was hearing! A break-out! Convicts dead, wounded and, worse, on the loose. Three guards murdered, including Hopkins. But perhaps it was a good job the man was dead, for what the hell had the fool been doing to allow it to happen?

The guards who had brought him the unwelcome news watched apprehensively as the man's face darkened in fury. Hard men, they were nevertheless frightened of facing his wrath and getting all the blame for the break-out.

Apart from calling them all the names under the sun, Bright didn't intend to waste valuable time in venting his anger on them, not yet anyway. That could come later. He was thinking what to do, wondering if he could hush the escape up. Well, the answer was probably not. Heads would surely roll for it, but his was not going to be one of them. In fact, he decided, it would be wisest to alert the authorities straightaway. They would expect that.

And in the meantime he'd try to minimize the damage as best he could. Although indolent for the most part, willing to let others do all the work while he took all the profit, at times he could act quickly and decisively. This was one of those times.

'OK. I don't know how it happened. At the moment I don't want to know. I just want it put right. Understand?'

The guards looked at one another, looked back at Bright and nodded.

'Divide the remaining guards into

four groups. One group to remain here to keep an eye on the prisoners we have still got. In fact it'd be a good idea to lock them in their cells and keep 'em there till things are back to normal. I don't want them causing trouble.'

'They won't like that.'

'Dammit all to hell and back, I don't give a damn about their feelings!' Bright took a deep breath, controlling his temper. 'Another group should bring in the dead and wounded, and the other two go after the runaways. Make sure they're well armed with plenty of ammunition. And make sure they understand I won't mind if they have to shoot first and ask any goddamned questions afterwards.'

'Yes, sir.'

'Good. Well, don't just stand there, get out of my sight. Get some rest — but tell the others I want results and I want them quickly.'

* * *

The telegraph operator thrust open the door to the marshal's office and stepped inside. Judd looked up.

'Mr Judd.' The operator waved a piece of paper at the marshal. 'This just came for you. All the way from Phoenix.'

It had to be important for the man to bring it himself. His first job perhaps? With a suddenly dry mouth Judd took the message, wondering where he was being sent, and what he was being instructed to do.

6

'Uh-oh,' Cameron said.

'What's up?'

'Riders! Look! Comin' after us.' Rob pointed along their back trail, where it was possible to make out a thin spiral of dust rising up into the still air.

'Dammit.' Hayes swore long and loudly. Pursuit had come faster than he'd hoped.

The riders — a posse of guards for sure — were still a long way away. But with fresh horses they'd catch up fast. Hayes stared ahead. Could they reach the foothills before that happened? He doubted it. Not with a nag that was already halfway to being played out, and two men on foot. And out here in the desert with nowhere to hide they were sitting targets.

Nearer was the Colorado. To go there would take them out of their way but along its banks or in the water they should find a hiding place.

By the time they reached the river it was early evening. The dust column was getting ever closer, and the three men were exhausted. They couldn't go on any further. They'd have to make their stand here.

But seeing the broken terrain, Hayes thought he'd made the right decision. And the dusk would give them an added advantage, make it more difficult for the guards to see and follow their trail.

This time of the year the Colorado was running fast and high. Hayes doubted they could cross it safely or quickly. It wouldn't do to get caught in the middle. Best to remain on this side, keep amongst the rocks, use twigs to brush away evidence of their passage.

Cameron and Murdoch didn't need to be told what to do — they were as used as Hayes to escaping posses.

Getting off the horse, Hayes led it down to the water's edge, then turned to walk along the wet sand. Quickly, the other two grabbed up handfuls of the bushes that grew by the banks and followed, sweeping the branches behind them and obliterating the tracks.

After a while they all looked back, well satisfied. Their trail was hard to distinguish. With luck, the members of the posse wouldn't be good trackers, and would believe their quarry had gone into the Colorado.

Pulling the horse after him, Hayes climbed over some rocks. On the farther side the bank sloped gently into the river, and for a while they were able to walk in the water. Up ahead was a larger stand of boulders. If they could reach that without being seen they might find a good place to hide.

'Hurry!' Murdoch suddenly said, in a voice full of urgency. 'I can hear the bastards.'

'Up here.' Hayes had spotted a large crevice between two rocks. Would it be big enough to hide the three of them and the horse? Perhaps he should have left the animal behind.

Quickly Cameron, with the revolver and six shots, climbed to the top of the rocks, leaving Hayes and Murdoch alone with the horse.

Hayes let out the breath he was holding as he realized there was plenty of room for them. Reaching into the saddlebag for more ammunition for the rifle, he pushed the horse out of the way. Leaving Murdoch to keep the animal quiet, he lay down on the ground, pointing the rifle downstream. One thing was certain — surrender was not an option. He doubted whether the posse would let them surrender anyway. Warden Bright, the bastard, had probably given orders to shoot on sight.

'Quiet!' Cameron called in warning. 'They're comin'. Oh hell, Ted, as far as I can see there are only four of the bastards.'

Four! Hayes almost laughed. He and Rob could easily handle four guards, no problem. If he'd known, he wouldn't have bothered hiding. Now he hoped they would come close enough so they could be dealt with.

They didn't.

Knowing the guards at Yuma, Hayes thought their hearts were in the chase, excited by the possibility of shooting and killing some of the escaped convicts, especially as he was one of them. But it was obvious that, unfortunately for them they weren't any good at following a trail once the tracks disappeared. Probably they were also apprehensive now it was getting dark, thinking their quarry could be any-where — perhaps even lying in ambush for them.

The four men came to a halt by the side of the water, staring up and down the banks. They even tried to cross the river. The Hayes gang watched as they argued and pointed and argued some more, a couple clearly wanting to go on — but go on where? — and a couple wanting to go back; but none of them liking the thought of returning empty-handed to Warden Bright.

In the end they gave up and rode away.

'Silly sons of bitches,' Hayes said. He stood up, hawked and spat. 'Well, boys, it looks like we're gonna be safe. Even so, we'd better keep goin', don't wanna take any chances.' He ignored the others' groans of protest. 'And it'll be cooler travelling at night.'

$\star$ $\star$ $\star$

In the morning they saw the ranch.

They'd travelled all night. All three were now afoot, the horse had long since played out and they'd left it behind. No water remained in the canteen. They were badly in need of horses, a change of clothes so they wouldn't be readily identified as con-victs, a wash, food and something — preferably whisky — to drink.

'And, boys,' Hayes said, 'that's where we're likely to find it all.'

Below them, nestling in a small valley, was an adobe ranch house, with a corral out front in which four sleek horses grazed, and a barn across the way. No sign of any bunkhouse, making it a family-run place.

'It's unlikely anyone there will offer us any real resistance.'

As they watched, crouched down amongst the bushes, the door to the house opened and a pretty girl of about sixteen came out.

Cameron grinned. 'Ain't all we're gonna get there, by the looks of things.'

'And after we can be on our way. Do what we want in our own time. Ain't no one else to come after us.'

7

Jubal Judd approached Yuma Prison with some dismay and disgust. He could hardly believe it. This — coming to this godawful place to chase after escaped convicts — was his first assignment.

Their re-capture, with the Mexican border so near, seemed unlikely. He wondered if he'd been deliberately chosen for the job so he would fail — and hoped not. Especially as he could see himself failing, after spending several hot and uncomfortable days riding across the desert.

He was also aware that Warden Bright would probably prefer to handle his dirty linen in private, and wouldn't be pleased to see him. Would give him little or no help. Well, he in turn didn't want to meet and help the Warden.

During Bright's time at Yuma, there

had been numerous complaints about his ill-treatment of prisoners, with rumours of deaths and suicides. Judd didn't believe in making life easy for convicts, who were, after all, proven guilty of various crimes, and in prison to learn the error of their ways. At the same time, he didn't approve of unnecessary brutality.

Somehow, Bright always managed to convince the powers that be that such treatment was justified. Judd felt it was not so much to do with Bright's excuse that convicts were more dangerous and violent than ever before, and so deserved such punishment — indeed, Bright maintained that was the only way to keep them in line — but more to do with the bribes and pay-offs about which stories circulated.

Unfortunately Judd could do nothing about the man, or his position. Except ask him a lot of awkward questions about how and why the break-out had happened. Watching Bright squirm as he tried to put the blame on everyone else but himself gave Judd a great deal of satisfaction, especially as Bright had made clear his contempt for Judd as soon as he'd seen him.

'Are there any of them still free?'

'Unfortunately, yes.'

'How many?'

'Five,' Bright answered confidently. At least he hoped it was five. His records weren't exactly up-to-date. There could well be several more men out there for whom he was unable to account — but what Judd didn't know, he couldn't use against the Warden. 'Naturally, I'm making every effort to ensure their re-capture. They can't get far. Not in the desert.' He nodded towards the window. 'My men will soon find them.'

'They've been free for well over twenty-four hours now,' Judd pointed out. 'They could be anywhere.'

Bright ignored this, saying instead, 'And two of them are no-accounts. Their escape was just an accident. They'll probably come to the gate any time now, begging to be let back in.'

Judd didn't think that very likely. 'What about the other three?'

Bright scowled, not wanting to admit to the escape of the Hayes gang, but seeing no way out of doing so. The marshal wouldn't go away before getting the answers he sought.

'Seems like I've heard of them,' Judd searched his memory. 'Weren't they responsible for a bank robbery down in Tucson a couple of years ago?'

'That's right. Two men were killed in it. A teller and a citizen in the street. Way it was told, they were shot down because Hayes felt like it. And, of course, that wasn't the first robbery, or murder, the gang had committed.'

'I wonder why they weren't hanged for it.'

Bright didn't have the answer to that, although he wished they had been. It would have saved him a lot of trouble.

'Was Hayes responsible for the break-out?'

'No. He just took advantage of the situation. And the bastard did shoot dead one of the guards. He's been a troublemaker since his arrival here. My men went after him, but they lost him down by the Colorado.'

Judd remembered Bright's earlier boast. 'I thought you said your men would have no problem in catching up with the escapees. It doesn't sound like it to me.'

Bright went red and swallowed hard to keep a hold on his temper. 'Hayes is a crafty bastard and he obviously knows a thing or two about faking a trail. I admit with luck on his side he could well get away.'

He might, but then Judd knew a thing or two about following a trail. 'Perhaps you'd better leave it to me.'

That suited Bright. Then he could find some way of holding this long-haired dandy responsible if the Hayes gang weren't re-captured — which seemed only too likely.

'Seems strange to me that you

allowed all three members of the gang to go out on the same work detail.'

'I didn't,' Bright lied, ever ready to lay the blame on someone who couldn't defend himself. 'That was Hopkins's own idea. I didn't know what he'd done until it was too late. I hoped it would be all right, but of course it wasn't.'

'Any idea where they'd go?'

Bright shrugged and said as if it was obvious, 'The border I suppose. Their first need will be to find water and food.'

'And will the gang stick together?'

'Hayes and Cameron will. They're friends from way back. Where one goes so does the other. I don't know about Murdoch. He might decide to go his own way.'

'Whereabouts on the Colorado did the guards lose the trail?'

Bright stood up and went over to a large map pinned to the wall. 'Somewhere in this area.'

Unable to think of anything else

useful he'd get out of the Warden, Judd stood up. 'Thanks for your time.'

Bright followed him to the door. 'Are you going after Hayes and the other two on your own?'

'Yeah,' Judd noticed Bright didn't offer for any of the guards to ride with him — he would have refused anyway.

'Then I wish you luck. They're all killers, so be careful.' But it was clear Bright meant neither sentiment. Wringing his hands together he added mournfully, 'I don't want them to get away. I lost three good men who were only doing their jobs, including Hopkins, my chief guard.'

'And it won't look good on your record, either.'

Bright drew himself up to his full height, and said indignantly, 'I'm not worried about that.' Although of course he was.

Outside in the yard, Judd mounted his horse. Several convicts, chained, helpless, beaten, watched him. Eyes looking firmly ahead, he rode past several newly dug graves, out of the gate and into the desert. He sighed with relief. Hot, thirsty and dusty he might be: he was also free.

8

Using the well-travelled road running along by the river, it took Glen Kramer over two hours to drive the buckboard into town. Antelope Wells was the sort of small town, and its inhabitants the sort of people, that once, not so long ago, he would have despised and wanted nothing to do with.

Go-ahead, bustling, full of its own self-importance, it was situated in a grassy valley with pine-clad hills all round. On the stagecoach route between Flagstaff and Tucson, stages called each day. Beyond the business district was a central plaza lined with stores, a café, a bank and a real estate office. There was a hotel. Down a side street stood the marshal's office and a small courthouse. The place boasted a church and a school, street lighting and well-kept sidewalks.

Yes indeed, as people were fond of telling Glen, Antelope Wells was a town going places. And Glen found he was glad to be part of it.

Although he reached the town early in the morning, having left the farm as soon as he'd eaten breakfast, the streets were already crowded. He drove by the livery stable and warehouses, and through the tiny red light district — two saloons, one brothel and a dancehall — which he'd never once been tempted to visit. In the plaza, horses and wagons were tied up in front of each store. Men hurried about their business, and women were shopping and gossiping.

Several people raised their hands in greeting. And as he pulled up outside MacKenzie's Dry Goods Store, both Mr MacKenzie and Max Sunderland, the town marshal, came out to greet him. Once upon a time Glen would most definitely have not wanted anything to do with any kind of lawman — would have avoided the man entirely. But, despite his responsible position,

Max wasn't a great deal older than Glen, and he and his wife, Betty, had become particular friends of Glen and Leonie.

'Hi!' Max greeted him. 'Thought you'd be in soon. Where's that pretty wife of yours?'

'I had to leave her back at the farm. There's so much to do at this time of the year.'

'Well, you're doing OK if all this is anything to go by.' MacKenzie was looking at the various kinds of vegetables loaded in the rear of the wagon. He nodded in satisfaction. 'I suppose you want me to buy everything?'

'I'd be pleased if you would.'

'Don't sound so anxious,' Sunderland advised. 'Pretend you don't care one way or the other and Mr MacKenzie will give you more'n he'll offer if he thinks you're desperate to sell to him.'

'That ain't true, Max, and you know it! And luckily so does Glen, don't you son?'

'Yessir.'

'Then you climb on down and come inside and we'll fix up a fair price without any unwanted interference from anyone else.'

'That's put me in my place,' Sunderland grinned. He banged Glen on the back. 'I'd better be going. Be sure and call in on me before you leave and I'll take you home for a piece of Betty's apple pie. She'll give me hell iffen I don't.'

'Wouldn't miss it for the world,' Glen said, adding loyally to himself that, however good Betty's pie was, it wouldn't be nearly as tasty as those Leonie baked.

The pungent smell of herbs, tobacco and a myriad of other things filled Glen's nose as he followed MacKenzie into the store. It was almost impossible to move about, so crowded was it with groceries, vegetables, household goods, farming equipment and horse harnesses. A way had to be picked through the piles of goods on the floor, to a

70

counter that seemed to groan beneath the weight of the articles stacked upon it.

Mrs MacKenzie, as plump and red-faced as her husband was thin and pale, waved to Glen and bustled off to fix them all up some coffee. Usually, at some time during the day, several women would gather round her, listening to the talk of the town, while old men sat near the stove in the corner, smoking and telling tall tales.

'Right, son,' MacKenzie pushed a jar of liquorice to one side and leant on the counter. 'You let me know what you've got to sell and I'll let you know what I'm willing to pay.'

'OK, sir.'

★　★　★

Max Sunderland strolled around the town, stopping to talk to some of its citizens. He knew that many of them thought that, at twenty-five, he was too young to do the job of town marshal.

That it should have gone to Arthur King, who had been the deputy for years. But King knew his limitations — he was a good deputy but didn't want the responsibility of leadership — and harboured neither ambitions nor grudges.

Not that, Sunderland admitted to himself, there was a great deal of responsibility involved — nor danger.

Collecting taxes, rounding up stray dogs, locking up the odd drunk — that was about it. Even the red light district caused few problems. Cowboys who wanted to be rowdy went to Flagstaff. While fist fights were reasonably common, he couldn't remember the last time anyone had pulled a gun.

At times he allowed himself a moment's discontent. He hadn't become a lawman to undertake such mundane duties. He wished for a bit more excitement. Wished something would happen so he could act quickly and earn people's respect. Unfortunately that didn't seem likely.

He sometimes wondered about moving on, but Betty liked it here — it was where she had lived all her life — and so did he, most of the time. And the town was growing, no doubt about that. There was even talk about a railroad spur being put in. It seemed right to be here from the beginning, knowing people, gaining a reputation for reliability — such things could stand him in good stead for the future.

In its own way the marshal's office was as crowded as Mr MacKenzie's store. Like most of the town's other buildings, it was built of adobe and had a false front protruding over the sidewalk, offering welcome shade. There was a barred window on either side of the door. Inside were two desks and chairs, for marshal and deputy, a stove for boiling coffee and a small table. The walls were covered with 'WANTED' posters. At the back, a door led through to four cells.

Eager to put aside the paperwork he was meant to be doing, Sunderland looked up as Glen came in. 'All done?'

'Yeah.' Glen appeared very pleased with himself.

It had been a good morning. Despite a lot of dickering and moaning, MacKenzie had paid a more than fair price for the vegetables. Glen had been able to buy food, some more seeds and a present for Leonie — some pink and yellow ribbons she could use to decorate the front of her otherwise plain dresses. The rest he'd put in the bank. Glen gave a secret smile at the thought of actually putting money *in* a bank, and not trying to take money out by robbing the place.

'I can't stay long,' he said, anxious to get home.

'Let me finish up here, be about ten minutes, and then we'll go on to see Betty. By the way, the church is holding a social Saturday week, d'you think you and Leonie can get in for it? You can stay with us afterwards rather than go all the way back home.'

'OK, yeah, thanks. Leonie will like

that.' As for himself, Glen wasn't so sure. He was still uncomfortable around a lot of people, scared one of them would know about his past. And he'd never mastered the art of dancing.

As the two men left the jailhouse, the stagecoach from Flagstaff pulled to a halt at the far side of the plaza.

Sunderland pulled his watch from its pocket. 'On time again. Umm . . . looks like something's up,' he added, as he saw a number of people gathering around the coach listening to the driver, a regular on the route. 'I'd better go and see what's happened. Come on.'

As they got to the stagecoach, Arthur King swung round to the marshal. 'There's been an escape from Yuma.'

Sunderland felt slightly disappointed. While he hadn't wanted anyone to be hurt, he had harboured a hope that the stage had been robbed and he could ride out looking for the thieves. An escape from Yuma was unusual, and therefore news, but it was unlikely to affect either him or Antelope Wells.

'Hope they don't come here,' he heard a woman say.

'No reason why they should,' her husband reassured her.

And Sunderland believed the same. Yuma wasn't really that near. And it was much more likely that the convicts would head for Mexico. Still he'd best show willing and take it seriously. So with Glen close behind him, not noticing that the young man had gone pale, he pushed his way to the front of the crowd.

Feeling very important, waving his arms around, the driver was saying, 'Apparently most of the bastards, beg pardon ladies, were shot or have been caught, but five of the bastards, beg pardon, escaped into the foothills.'

'Any idea who they were?' Sunderland asked.

'A John Gutteridge and an Arnold Daily. Two no-accounts. And the Hayes gang, remember them? They robbed the bank down in Tucson, killed a couple of

men while they were at it. Hayes,
Cameron and Murdoch . . . '

The driver went on but Glen no
longer heard him.

'Oh, Jesus Christ,' he whispered to
himself. 'Oh, Christ, no.'

All his worst nightmares had come
true.

9

Glen had run away from home when he was fifteen, a year after his widowed mother had married a man determined to beat the devil out of his step-son.

It had seemed only natural to leave the farmlands of Iowa behind and head west. He'd meant to become a cowboy, but in the deserts of New Mexico and Arizona it was easier by far to join with other wild youngsters in rustling cows and robbing trader's stores. Herding cattle for other people was hard, boring work for little reward. This way, there was excitement, easy money and, given the vast empty spaces and the lack of lawmen, not much danger.

All that had led in turn to him joining the Hayes gang.

To be part of a gang actually known to, and wanted by, the law had been thrilling.

At first.

It hadn't taken Glen long to realize his mistake.

Hayes and Cameron both were ruthless, quite ready to kill — not merely to escape the law, but for the sport and pleasure of it. And Murdoch went along with them, being too lazy to do anything else.

There was also a great deal of difference between robbing country stores and lone travellers, where little resistance was encountered, to robbing banks and stagecoaches. More than once they'd been shot at and pursued by a posse of outraged citizens.

'A hazard of the trail,' Hayes said, laughing, as if dodging bullets was something to be enjoyed.

Not wanting to be mocked for being scared, Glen hadn't dared object. But he had been scared. And worried. He didn't want to shoot anyone, which he might be forced to do. And neither did he want to be shot, perhaps killed, or be caught and sent to jail for a long time — which would surely be the outcome for any member of the notorious Hayes gang.

He wanted to leave the gang, but doubted whether Hayes would let him. Apart from Cameron, and to a certain extent Murdoch, Hayes didn't trust, or like, anyone. He might suspect Glen would betray him to the law. If so, the man would surely prefer to leave him in the desert with a bullet in his back rather than allow him to ride away.

In the end Glen's chance of escape had come when they'd robbed the bank in Tucson.

It had seemed a risky proposition to Glen, seeing as the bank was situated right in the middle of a busy plaza. Even Cameron had doubts. No one was likely to take any notice of Glen, and Hayes had talked Cameron out of his misgivings.

The robbery had gone ahead.

Just after two o'clock, they'd ridden into the plaza. Because it was so hot not many people were around. They'd

80

dismounted and left their horses tied to the rail outside the café, crossed the dusty road, gone into the bank.

Inside it was dim and cool, windows shuttered against the afternoon sun. Three tellers were busy behind the counter, and a few customers, men and women, waited their turn to be served. On one wall a clock ticked noisily.

At Hayes's shout, and faced with four men wielding guns, there had been no resistance from the bank staff or the suddenly terrified customers who obediently lay face down on the floor. While Ted and Glen held guns on the tellers who stuffed sacks with dollar bills, Murdoch covered the bank's manager as he sat at his desk in an inner office, and Cameron stood at the door ready to deal with anyone who came in.

Things were going well. Glen thought they were going to get away with it.

He wasn't sure what happened. What went wrong.

One minute he and Hayes were

collecting the heavy sacks of money. The next Hayes cried out angrily and fired his gun. The teller nearest to him immediately fell to the floor, a bloody hole appearing in his forehead.

Surely the man hadn't tried to raise the alarm? There was no sign of a gun. Glen believed it much more likely he had taken too long in handing over his sack, or had annoyed Hayes in some other mysterious way. So Hayes shot him for the hell of it. It wouldn't be the first time.

Whatever it was, pandemonium broke out, both inside and outside the bank. Cameron joined in the shooting, without actually hitting anyone. People screamed.

'Let's get outta here!' Murdoch yelled.

In the dash for the door Hayes dropped a bag of the money, while Glen somehow kept a hold on the two sacks he held.

And outside, following the cry 'The bank's being robbed!', guns had been unholstered by angry townsmen and were held ready to be fired as soon as the robbers emerged. They'd had to shoot their way to the horses. Another man was killed, and Hayes was wounded in the arm.

A determined posse, led by a determined marshal, had followed them into the mountains.

Somehow there, in the darkness and confusion, Glen slipped away. He hadn't planned it, but when the opportunity presented itself he'd seized it — to be free of the gang, free of the threat of being caught. And after he'd gone, he realized he still had the two sacks of money tied to the saddle.

From a high vantage point in the rocks, he'd watched the other three men as they were cornered by the posse. They made a fight of it, but in the end they were easily captured. Taken back to Tucson.

Glen had ridden all night and by morning it was obvious no one was coming after him. Perhaps in all the confusion they didn't even know about him. As far as he knew he hadn't been part of the gang long enough for his face to appear on a 'WANTED' poster.

Whatever the reason he was free and clear. And he had fifty thousand dollars of stolen money, with which he could do anything and go anywhere.

★　★　★

'Shouldn't you tell Marshal Sunderland?' Leonie asked, clutching Glen's hands as they sat side by side at the kitchen table. Her face had whitened with fear and she was trembling. 'Warn him Hayes might come here.'

'I don't know.' Glen pulled away from her and went to the window, looking out at the evening sky. 'I don't see how Hayes can find out where I am. And will he bother? Won't he be more concerned to escape to Mexico? I know I would be.' He sighed. Hayes wasn't like other men. 'If I really believed he'd come here of course I'd tell Max, warn

84

him, take the consequences, but I might be telling him for no reason. And if I do tell him, he'll have to do something about it.'

'Arrest you, you mean? Would he do that?'

'Max might be my friend, he's also a lawman.'

'But you sent the money back.'

'I don't think that'd make a whole helluva lot of difference. Two men were killed, remember?'

'You didn't shoot them.'

'I was there. And Tucson wasn't the only robbery I was involved in.'

'Oh, Glen, how on earth did they escape?'

Glen shrugged. 'These things happen.'

Leonie joined her husband at the window. 'Are you sure they won't find you?'

'No I'm not sure. But how can they?' Glen paused then went on. 'But, just in case, perhaps you should go into town and stay with the Sunderlands.'

'No!' Leonie said sharply. 'Whatever happens, my place is here by your side.'

'You don't know what Hayes and the others are like. What they're capable of.'

'I don't care. I'm not going to leave you.'

'All right. I won't try and make you.'

Leonie turned away so Glen wouldn't see the fear in her eyes. She wished with all her heart that Hayes and the others hadn't escaped. She wouldn't rest easily until she'd heard they'd been recaptured — or preferably shot and killed.

Until then she would spend every minute being afraid. But all the same, nothing and no one would chase her away from her home. Or from Glen.

10

It didn't take Jubal Judd long to find the place where the convicts' break-out had occurred. The ground was broken and scuffed, blood had seeped into the sand and no one had bothered to move or even bury the dead mule, whose body was already host to scavengers.

Warden Bright's two no-account prisoners had run off into the desert, seeming to confirm the fact they weren't too clever. But Hayes and his companions had done the sensible thing and headed for the foothills.

It was easy to follow their trail: one ridden horse, two men afoot. Easy to see where the posse of guards had given chase, and where the gang veered off its course and fled for the Colorado.

Once there it was no longer so easy, and Judd could see how the guards had lost the trail and given up. The gang was clever. They'd scuffed out their sign, and could have gone into the water to the opposite bank, or ridden up or downriver.

It took Judd several hours of patient searching to find the tracks again, but find them he did. Leading away from the Colorado. And after a quick cup of coffee and some sourdough biscuits, he set out to follow. The men, sure there would be no pursuit, hadn't bothered to hide their trail.

Well, Judd thought, that was his gain and their misfortune.

⋆ ⋆ ⋆

'How long till we get to Nita?' Cameron asked, taking off his stolen Stetson and running his hands through his hair.

'Not long. Day or two I reckon,' Hayes said. It could be quicker, but it was so hot they were taking it easy, not rushing.

'Supposing she ain't there?' Murdoch said.

Hayes gritted his teeth. He was getting fed up and angry with Murdoch's bitching. He should be grateful. Weren't for him and Cameron, Murdoch would still be suffering in Yuma. 'She will be. Where the hell else would a whore like her go?'

'She might have gone off with Glen. With all that money they could afford to go anywhere together.'

Hayes frowned. He hadn't thought of that. 'She'd damn well better not have done!'

Wanting to avoid an explosion of temper, Cameron quickly said, 'We'll find out soon enough now.' He thought it wouldn't augur well for the Dawsons if Nita had left; not if the look on Hayes's face was anything to go by.

★ ★ ★

Judd had a bad feeling as he rode down the track to the small ranch. Although well-looked-after with smoke rising from its one chimney, the place had a

89

deserted air, with no one about and no horses in the corral. And earlier the Hayes gang had spent some time on the hill above the ranch, clearly watching it.

'Hallo!' he called out, but no one replied.

And as soon as he reached the house, he realized his disquiet was justified. The door was open, and beyond it he could see the unmoving body of a man.

Judd got off his horse and drew one of his guns. He didn't think Hayes was still here, but he wasn't about to take any chances. Using the gun barrel, he pushed the door further open and took a cautious step inside.

The man had been shot, several times. He was the lucky one.

The other three bodies were in the parlour: a young man of about eighteen, who was tied to a chair and who'd been beaten up and otherwise tortured; and two women — one in her forties, the other no more than a girl. The gang had had some fun with both women, probably making the boy watch what they did to his mother and sister, before killing all three.

The place was looted and what couldn't be taken was broken.

The family, all alone, not expecting trouble, hadn't stood a chance when the Hayes gang came calling.

Judd didn't waste time in cursing the men or wondering what kind of animals they were. Instead, clamping down on his anger, he went outside and got on with digging graves to bury the bodies. The sooner he did that, the sooner he could be on his way, after the three killers. They now had food, a change of clothes and horses. But catch up with them he would.

★ ★ ★

The camp was small and untidy. Hayes and Murdoch sprawled by the remains of the fire, moaning about how hot and dusty it was, how they wanted some whisky and women, wondering when they would leave the desert behind.

Cameron left them to it. They were free of Yuma, and with any luck at all, about to get their hands on a lot of money, while avenging themselves on the kid: surely that was worth a bit of discomfort.

He climbed to the top of the ridge where they'd stopped. And came to a sudden halt. What he saw he didn't like. He slithered and slid back down.

'Ted!'

Hayes looked up, suddenly alert. 'What is it?'

'We've got company.'

'The guards from Yuma?' Murdoch asked. 'How the hell could they follow us all this way?'

Cameron shook his head. 'Nope. Not them. Looks like just one man to me.'

'Could be a cowboy or some other traveller,' Hayes suggested.

'With a badge glinting on his chest?'

'Hell!'

The three men hurried to the top of the slope. The rider was already a lot closer, riding slowly but purposefully along their trail. After them for sure.

Hayes spent several minutes swearing at lawmen in general, and the rider in particular.

Cameron didn't say anything about it being Hayes's fault for allowing them to take such a slow pace, and for not hiding their tracks because he was sure they were safe — that would be to risk having the man turn his temper on him!

Instead he said, 'Where the hell did he come from? Who is he?'

With no answer to either question, Hayes said, 'What does it matter?' He raised the rifle that was never far from his side.

'What you goin' to do?' Murdoch asked.

'Shoot the sonofabitch.' And Hayes pulled the trigger.

A few seconds later the three men whooped in delight as rider and horse fell to the ground.

Then with a note of disappointment, Cameron said, 'Hell, Ted, lookee there. You got his horse, not him.'

'The bastard can't run far. Let's get after him.'

* * *

The shot came out of nowhere. And the next thing Judd knew, his horse let out a squeal of pain and collapsed forward on its knees, sending him sprawling over its head.

As he climbed quickly to his feet, Judd gave a grunt of disgust, knowing he'd been careless. It had soon become obvious that the Hayes gang weren't heading for Mexico. Instead, to his surprise, they seemed to be riding north. They weren't moving all that quickly either. Anxious both not to lose them, and to catch up as soon as he could, he hadn't bothered to read the signs beyond merely following the trail.

His carelessness had almost cost him his life. Could still do so.

His horse was dead. He was left on foot. Doubtless the outlaws would be coming to finish what they'd started. Of course, he could shoot it out with them, might even get one or two before they killed him, but that wasn't good enough. Not after the things they'd done. He wanted all three: dead or alive.

His best bet was to hide. Live to fight another day.

Without pausing Judd took to his heels, racing towards a distant clump of mesquite bushes and cottonwood trees by an outcropping of rocks. By the time he got there he could hear the pounding of horses' hooves.

He had no chance to find a hiding place in the rocks. All he could do was crawl in amongst the bushes, ignoring their scratching of his hands and face, and duck down.

And there he lay, clutching his two Colts, heart beating fast, watching as the three men rode up and brought their horses to a halt nearby.

'Hell, where's he gone?' Cameron peered at the bushes. 'He came this way, didn't he?'

'The bastard is in there, somewhere, hiding, watching us,' Hayes said.

'Yeah, and mebbe gettin' ready to shoot us.' Murdoch sounded nervous.

'He can't get all of us.' Why was Murdoch forever urging caution? It was beginning to smack of cowardice.

'Come closer,' Judd urged silently. If they did he would be certain of getting off three good shots with his Colt; of downing them all. At the moment they were just out of range. In firing he would succeed only in giving his position away. If only he'd managed to grab up his rifle — the bastards would be dead then!

'Harvey's right,' Cameron said, scared Hayes would take it into his head to ride in amongst the bushes just for the hell of it. 'He's a lawman, we're escaped prisoners, he'd be justified.'

Hayes swore. 'I don't like damn lawmen. We oughta go after this one, shoot him, make sure he can't follow us any more.'

'The bastard could at this very moment be lining us up in his sights, ready to pick us off one at a time. He does, we'll never get back at Glen.'

Murdoch added, 'Risks are all very well, Ted, but not when they're stupid.'

'After all,' Cameron went on, 'what's the point? What can he do? He's afoot, out here in the middle of goddamned nowhere. I reckon he'll be dead soon enough, or so far behind us it won't make no nevermind.'

'OK,' Hayes agreed reluctantly, 'Sure wish I'd shot the sonofabitch though.'

As the three men rode away, Judd unhappily had to agree with Cameron.

Although he'd had no choice, letting them go like that didn't set right, especially as it might result in their escape. For he was stuck out here in the desert, without a horse, and wearing uncomfortable, high-heeled boots.

Judd got to his feet with a sigh. He'd go back to the poor horse, get the saddle, canteen of water and his rifle, and then start walking. He started ahead at the flat, uncompromising desert.

Hell, whoever said being a lawman was an easy occupation?

11

The saloon and brothel run by Mabel and Jack Dawson stood near a water-hole, sheltered by cypress trees and overlooked by a sandy slope. Isolated on the edge of the desert, it was a wonder not only that anyone ever found the place, but that anyone lived or worked close by enough to visit it. Yet the customers kept the greedy Dawsons happy, and they employed a bartender and three whores.

And of the three whores, Nita was the prettiest and most popular.

With her last customer having left her bed, the girl sat in front of the mirror in her room, combing out the long black hair that hung almost to her waist. As the daughter of a poor Mexican girl and an American sheepherder, she had her mother's dark eyes and dark skin, but like her father she was tall and slim.

As their daughter, she'd never intended to have a life as hard and unrewarding as theirs.

She had become a prostitute at fifteen. Now, ten years later, she often wondered if, in fact, her life was any better than her mother's. She owned little of her own, just a few ornaments to brighten up this room. Everything else — furniture, clothes and make-up — belonged to Mabel Dawson. No money saved. Little in the future to look forward to.

Yet what else could she have done? She had no education, no skills. Had known nothing but how to use her body.

It certainly didn't fulfil her girlish dreams of making a home for a handsome husband and several children. Only once had she met someone she thought she might have that with, and that was when Glen Kramer came to the brothel with the rest of the Hayes gang. She remembered seeing him for the first time. How handsome she'd considered him; how, later, she'd realized his arrogant bluster hid uncertainty. Remembered sitting on the porch talking to him about their families, and how both of them had come to be at this place at this time.

It hadn't worked out between them, and, like all the other men, Glen had moved on. And she was still working for Mabel Dawson, in this godforsaken spot, and probably would be forever more; or at least until her looks faded and she was no longer sought out.

★ ★ ★

'There it is,' Hayes said, as the three men came to a halt on the slope overlooking the saloon. 'Ain't changed at all, has it?'

They'd all enjoyed several nights of pleasure here, for the Dawsons didn't mind what their customers did for a living so long as they paid.

It was mid-morning. The best and safest time of day. When the clients would have left for home, and the girls would be sleeping off their night's work.

Even so, Hayes wasn't taking any chances. It was just possible that the law knew about Nita, and was setting a trap here. So they'd wait a while and watch. But not too long, because it would be good to enjoy some willing women, have a drink or two.

'It looks OK to me,' Cameron said after a while, getting impatient. 'Just a couple of horses in the corral, and they probably belong to the Dawsons. Let's go on down.'

'OK,' Hayes agreed.

* * *

Jack Dawson, a plump man with brown hair turning grey, saw the men slowly riding towards the ever open door of the saloon. He called Mabel and she, also plump and greying, hurried to the front of the brothel. Her eyes lit up. Customers calling during the day!

She clapped her hands and raised her

voice to a yell. 'Come on, girls, up you get! Look lively!'

Groaning and grumbling, for she'd just been going to sleep, Nita hastily put on her blue dress over her chemise, frilly drawers and high-heeled shoes. When Mabel demanded, she expected to be obeyed.

As Nita joined Daisy and Pauline at the top of the stairs, Hayes led the way into the cathouse's parlour.

Nita's eyes widened in disbelief and terror.

'What's the matter?' Daisy asked.

'It's trouble,' Nita said, clutching the other girl's hand.

Even as Nita recognized the gang so did Mabel Dawson, her hands going to her mouth. And swiftly Cameron pulled the revolver from the waistband of his trousers, making everyone except Nita cry out.

Hayes said, 'Good morning, ladies. We don't want no trouble here. Behave yourselves and there won't be none. Harve, go and round up any pilgrims in the saloon. Bring 'em in here. Hi there, Mrs Dawson, Nita, pleasure to see you both again. I see you're employing two new girls, and very nice they are too.'

'What do you want here?' Mabel demanded.

Hayes laughed. 'Why, to enjoy your girls, and to have a quiet word with Nita.'

'Leave me alone,' Nita said. 'I don't want anything to do with you.'

Thinking of her own skin, Mabel said, 'Don't be difficult.'

'That's right, Nita, be nice.' Hayes grinned. 'Now why don't you three lovely ladies come on down here? Let's have a good look at you.'

'It's all right,' Nita told her frightened companions. 'They won't hurt you.' Although she wasn't sure about that. Trying not to show anyone — friend or foe — how scared she was, she walked down the stairs ahead of Daisy and Pauline.

As they got to the bottom, Murdoch came in herding Dawson, the bartender and a grizzled old miner who'd been sleeping off a night's drinking in front of him.

'I see you've still got the piano in here.' Hayes nodded at the instrument in the corner. 'I suppose Jack plays it so the girls can dance to the music?'

'Yes, sir. Would you like me to play now? Or is there anything else I can do for you?'

'I don't think so. In fact, I think it would be better if all those people not necessary to our enjoyment were locked somewhere safe so they can't do nothin' stupid.'

'Don't hurt us,' Mabel moaned. 'We ain't never done you no harm.'

'I don't mean to. You provide so many comforts for your fellows that we'd be in all sorts of trouble if we deprived 'em. Surely you've got some place where you can be shut up?'

Dawson nodded. 'The cellar.' It seemed wisest to go along with what the men wanted.

'Good. Harve . . . '

'Yeah, I know, I know. I'll go and lock 'em up. Come on.'

'And bring back a couple of bottles,' Cameron added. 'Some of their real good sipping whisky.'

'Which lovely lady d'you want, Rob?'

'The fair one,' Cameron said. He grabbed Daisy, pulling her roughly into his arms, causing her to squeal. 'Show me upstairs, darlin'.'

'That leaves you for Harve.' Hayes nodded at the brown-haired girl. 'Wait for him here. He won't be long. I don't need to tell you not to do anythin' silly, do I?' Wordlessly Pauline shook her head. 'Good. Nita, you come with me.'

'What is it you want?'

'What do you think? First of all I'm goin' to make love to you, and then you're goin' to tell me where I can find Glen Kramer.'

Nita's heart sank. Ever since seeing the gang, that was the very thing she'd been scared of. For there could be no other reason for them to come all the way here.

Head held high, she walked up the stairs ahead of the man. What was she going to do? She was content to lie next to him in her bed, as if she was there willingly, but to betray Glen to him was different altogether. Yet Hayes had an ill temper, and was ruthless when he didn't get his own way; would willingly hurt or kill. Although she had no particular fondness for either of the Dawsons, she had no desire to see them come to harm. Daisy and Pauline were her friends, in the same position as she was.

And whatever she said, would she be able to convince him she didn't know where Glen was?

'You must have seen Glen after what happened down in Tucson,' Hayes said.

Nita nodded. 'He came here to tell me it all went wrong. He also said he was leaving the outlaw trail behind.'

That was when Nita hoped Glen would take her with him. She'd known almost from the first moment of meeting him that he wasn't really cut

107

out to be an outlaw — at least, not one belonging to the violent Hayes gang. He was the sort who, once he'd sowed his wild oats, would want a wife and family, not a long jail sentence. Unhappily for Nita, he hadn't wanted her to be that wife.

'Where was he goin'?'

'I don't know.'

'Nita!'

'No, it's true. He never said.'

'I dunno why you think you've gotta protect him, when he left you here to whore for anyone with the price. And I ain't sure I believe you.' He pinched her arm.

'Let me go, you're hurting!' Nita cried out as Hayes dragged her from the bed and shook her hard. 'Honestly, Ted, please. Why would he tell me? He didn't know where he was going himself.'

'Well, we'll just have to see about that won't we?'

'Don't hurt me. Please.'

But, of course, that was exactly what

108

Hayes did. He liked hurting people and he might have hit her anyway just for the fun of it. But as far as he was concerned to beat her was the best, the only way, to learn if she was lying to him. It was with some satisfaction that he found out she was.

'Please, Ted, no more,' Nita begged from the floor where his latest blow had sent her sprawling.

Blood seeped from her lips, one tooth was loose and her left eye was already bruised and closing. She had been beaten up before by drunken, angry men — it was one of the hazards of the job — but not like this. Hayes would carry on hitting her until he was satisfied she was telling the truth.

'Then where did he go?' he demanded, looming over her, one hand clutching her long hair, dragging her head up, forcing her to look at him.

'Flagstaff,' Nita sobbed. 'He said he was heading for Flagstaff.'

'And then what was he goin' to do?'

'I don't know. Really, I don't.'

'Sure?'

'Yes.'

'Never mind. I knew you'd be a good girl eventually. See how much easier it would've been if you'd told me what I wanted to know at the beginning. The bastard kid ain't worth protecting, really he ain't.' Hayes reached down and hauled her to her feet, ignoring her cry of pain. 'I wonder if Rob and Harve have finished. If so we can all be on our way can't we?'

A shiver of fear ran down Nita's spine. 'What do you mean?'

'You're comin' with us, didn't I tell you that?'

'No!' Nita's voice rose in fear.

'Don't pretend you like it here with Mabel Dawson. Wouldn't you rather come with us? We'll treat you real good.'

The trouble was Hayes believed what he said. He really thought that she would prefer to ride with him than stay

110

behind, even after the beating he'd just given her.

'Why do you want me with you?'

'Well, sweetheart, Glen always had a soft spot for you. Mebbe he still has. You'll be useful in making him do what he might otherwise not want to do. You see I reckon even if he don't love you, a silly son-ofabitch like him won't want to see you hurt.'

'No, Ted, please don't.'

Naturally Hayes took no notice, because his mind was made up. And while he didn't want to get caught with his pants literally down, he reckoned he had time to make love to Nita one more time before they left. Laughing he threw her onto the bed.

12

Judd had long since started to limp. His
feet were blistered, his legs ached and
so did his shoulder, from carrying the
heavy saddle. He'd run out of water.
Seen no one from whom to beg help.
His face and clothes were covered in
dust. Willpower alone kept him going.
And he was beginning to wonder how
long it would be before he couldn't go
on.

Then as he tramped along, studying
the ground, carefully putting one foot
in front of the other, he looked up and
saw the waterhole and the buildings.

They were so unexpected that he
came to a startled halt, wondering if he
was seeing things. Especially when the
door opened and two girls wearing
nothing but chemises, petticoats and
black stockings ran out to meet him.
Mirage or not, the sight of them

gladdened his heart and made him smile, even if their anxiety to reach him might have more to do with his badge than anything else.

For as they neared him they both cried out, 'Marshal! Marshal!'

When a plump, middle-aged couple followed the two girls, Judd knew who they were and where he was. He'd never visited Jack and Mabel Dawson, but he'd heard of them and their place of pleasure from various other lawmen. He'd reached safety.

'Hi, ladies,' he managed to say, his voice sounding gritty.

While the fair-haired prostitute grabbed at his arm, the second girl said, 'Are you all right? Here, let me take your saddle. Where have you come from? Come on, you look as if you could do with a drink.'

'Water first, followed by several beers,' Judd agreed.

'Anything else you want, sweetheart?' the fair girl asked saucily.

'I saw him first, Daisy.'

113

'I reached him first.'

While it was gratifying to have two pretty girls fighting over him, Judd felt it best to confess, 'Right now I'm too tired, honey, but after those beers . . . who knows?'

Daisy giggled.

As they neared the Dawsons, the girls helping him, Judd could see that what he'd taken for shutters across several of the windows in saloon and brothel were actually badly nailed-up boards.

Mabel Dawson hurried forward. 'Thank God you're here! We've been robbed. Our hospitality abused. You can see what it's been like.' She waved a hand at the broken, boarded up windows. 'We've had to turn people away.'

'And my bartender was shot for absolutely no good reason at all,' Jack Dawson added.

'Whoa up,' Judd protested. 'I've been walking out there in the desert for a helluva long time. I'm tired, everything aches. I could do with a drink, followed by a hot bath and a meal. And a comfortable chair to sit in. If you can do that for me, I can listen to all your troubles.'

'I'll look after you,' Daisy offered and, much to Pauline's annoyance, Mabel nodded her agreement.

* * *

Some time later Judd felt more like his old self. Rather better, in some ways, than he had for quite a while, as Daisy had looked after him very well indeed. And for all her faults, Mabel proved a good cook, putting before him a plate piled high with beef, potatoes, string beans and thick gravy. Jack Dawson's beer was frothy, cold and there was plenty of it.

Judd downed the last of the beer and pushed his chair back, sighing. 'That's better. Now then,' he surveyed the other four people sitting round the table watching him, 'what happened?'

'We had visitors,' Dawson said. 'The Hayes gang.'

That was hardly a surprise to Judd. 'When was this?'

'Three days ago.'

Dammit, Judd thought, after their run-in with him they must have got a move on. He didn't like it; they were too far ahead.

'You knew who they were?'

Mabel said, 'They used to come here sometimes. Before they were caught for that robbery down in Tucson. Nita was sweet on one of 'em.'

'Which one?'

'Glen Kramer.'

Judd felt puzzled. He'd never heard of anyone called Glen Kramer.

'He'd only recently joined the gang.' Dawson explined. 'That robbery occurred before any lawman heard about him. He wasn't on any of the 'WANTED' posters.'

'He was a nice boy,' Mabel went on. 'Too nice for that bastard, Hayes.'

'Hayes always was trouble. And Rob

Cameron weren't much better.'

'What did they come here for?'

'They wanted my girls for free; and they wanted Nita.'

'Poor Nita,' said Daisy, and both girls' eyes filled with tears.

Pauline said, 'Oh, Mr Judd, that bastard Hayes hurt her real bad. We could hear her crying and begging. He made her scream. And there weren't a thing we could do to help her. They locked everyone but me and Daisy in the cellar. And me and Daisy were with the other two. They threatened to shoot us if we tried to help Nita.' She shuddered. 'They would have done too.'

'I was with the young one, Rob,' said Daisy. 'I asked him to stop Hayes hitting Nita. He said he wanted to but he was scared of Hayes as well.' She shook her head. 'I didn't believe him. He liked listening to Nita crying. And he weren't all that gentle either! Not like you, sweetheart,' she added, squeezing Judd's arm.

'But what did they want with her? D'you know?'

'It musta been to do with that Glen Kramer,'

Dawson said. 'I reckon they're trying to find him.'

'Why?'

Mabel said, 'Glen came by here after the robbery to say goodbye to Nita. He'd run out on the gang, leaving them to get caught, and he had the bank's money with him.'

'So they'd want to find both him and the money and have their revenge on him?'

'Yeah.' Dawson nodded agreement. 'And they musta thought Nita knew where he went.'

It made sense of the fact that they hadn't run to Mexico. 'And did she?'

'Nita said he was going to head in the direction of Flagstaff,' Pauline said. 'See what happened when he got there. Sometimes she thought about going there too, trying to find him, but she never did.'

'And they took Nita, my poor girl, with them.' Mabel wiped at her eyes, which Judd thought probably hadn't shed real tears for many a year. 'I worry about her all the time and the things they might be doing to her.'

'She didn't want to go?'

'She most certainly did not!' Daisy protested indignantly.

'All right, sweetheart, I had to ask.'

Daisy smiled at Judd, forgiving him for his remark. 'She often spoke about how she hated them. How she was glad they were in jail where they couldn't hurt anyone. She said Glen was sorry he'd joined their gang and wanted to leave them, but didn't know how.'

Pauline went on, 'Mr Judd, Nita was halfway in love with Glen, and Hayes probably took her along to use as a weapon against him. Way Nita spoke, though Glen wasn't in love with her he was a gentleman. He wouldn't want Nita hurt.'

'And,' Judd turned to Dawson, 'they shot your bartender?'

'Yeah. As the bastards were riding away, the girls let us out of the cellar. By then they'd reached the top of the slope. They stopped and looked back and started firing, even though they were too far away for us to try and catch up. We all scattered for cover but not before the tender was shot in the shoulder. He ain't badly hurt but there was just no reason for it.'

'The reason, Mr Dawson, is that Hayes and the others enjoy hurting people.'

'They also shot out most of the windows and broke whatever bottles of whisky they couldn't take with them,' Mabel said.

'But I guess we were lucky. They could've taken it into their heads to shoot us all.'

'What are you going to do?' Mabel asked.

'Keep after 'em.'

'I hope you're good at what you do. You'll need to be to go up against Hayes.'

'Thanks for the warning,' Judd said, not feeling he needed one. 'Have you got a horse I can requisition?'

Dawson didn't look particularly pleased about that, obviously wondering if he'd ever be reimbursed for the animal. After being poked in the ribs by his wife, he said, 'Yeah, of course. We can set you up with some provisions as well. Help you on your way.'

And Mabel added, 'Get those bastards, and get my little Nita back. She's very dear to me. As are all my girls.'

Judd didn't take much notice of that.

'Will you be back this way?' Daisy asked, squeezing his hand.

Judd grinned. 'You never know, sweetheart, I just might come and visit you again.'

13

The worst thing, Glen thought, was not knowing whether the Hayes gang was still at large, or whether they'd been killed or re-captured. People might know in Antelope Wells, but he couldn't keep riding into town and asking. Everyone would wonder why, and it would mean leaving Leonie alone. He knew that his wife was very scared, despite her efforts to hide her fear from him.

Wanting to protect her, he took to wearing his gun strapped to his hip. It didn't do him any good when the Hayes gang arrived at the farm.

He had no warning. One minute he was weeding all alone in the field nearest to the river. The next, when he stood up, the three men were close by sitting on horses, watching him; and with them was Nita, one eye blackened, her lips swollen.

Glen's heart flipped over. And he found he was too frightened to do anything but stand still, looking at them.

'Hi, kid.' Hayes dismounted and stepped forward, reaching out to pluck Glen's gun from its holster. He grinned. 'Took us a time to find you. Bet you're surprised to see us. And, boy, ain't we surprised to see you, here on a farm, of all places! Never expected a real wild 'un like you would turn into a farmer.'

'Glen Kramer, sodbuster,' Cameron said with a little giggle. 'That is still the name you're using, ain't it? Or did you change it after you ran out on us?'

'Cat's got his tongue,' Hayes jeered. 'C'mon, kid, answer Rob.'

Glen found his voice at last. Hoping he didn't sound as frightened as he felt, he said, 'No, it's still Glen Kramer. And I didn't run out on you.'

'Didn't see you standing trial with us.'

'You didn't really expect me to give

myself up just because you'd been captured, did you?'

'I expected you to try and help us.'

'What, break you out of the Tucson jail?'

'D'you know what it was like in Yuma?' Cameron said, face reddening with sudden anger. 'Hellhole is what. We suffered there, boy.'

'Well, it doesn't matter now, does it?' Hayes draped an arm round Glen's shoulder squeezing hard until the young man winced. 'We're free and clear of the place and we've found our old pal. 'Course, Glen, you didn't make it easy for us to follow your trail, but we managed it, and now we're all together again. The Hayes Gang. And it's all thanks to young Nita there.'

Glen glanced at the girl again.

'I'm sorry, Glen, really,' she said, tears coming into her eyes. 'I didn't want to tell Ted. He made me.'

Glen nodded. He could see for himself Hayes' means of persuasion. He didn't blame Nita. 'What do you want here with me?'

'Want? Want? Why, like I said, nothing more than for the Hayes gang to ride again — '

'I ain't having anything more to do with you. That life is behind me now.'

'Like hell,' Cameron muttered.

' — and for our share of the money. Nita tells me it was somethin' like fifty thousand dollars. We've all been thinking about what we could do with so much money! And all we want is our share. You see, kid, I'm so generous I'm gonna let you keep your share. Probably.'

'But — '

Hayes interrupted him. 'Let's get on up to the house, kid. Meet this nice wife of yours.' He reached out, grabbing hold of Glen's arm, shoving him forward so he almost fell.

Glen wished there was some way he could warn Leonie, so she could try to get away. For who knew what Hayes and the others would do? Especially

125

when they learned the truth about the money. As it was, like Nita, he could do nothing but what Hayes told him. It was obvious the man was having difficulty keeping a rein on his temper, and it wouldn't take much for him to lose it. Then all hell would break loose.

Leonie was in the parlour, dusting, when the door opened. She looked up. And, with sinking heart, Glen watched her smile die and her eyes widen with fear as she saw the company with him. He wanted to go to her, to comfort her, but Murdoch stuck a gun in his side, stopping him.

As Leonie went to cry out, Rob Cameron leapt forward, pulling her close, putting a dirty hand over her mouth and nose so she could hardly breathe. It was quite unnecessary, there being no one to hear her.

'Leave her alone!' Glen yelled angrily. 'Don't you dare touch her!'

'Shut up,' Murdoch warned, prodding him with the gun.

Hayes gave Leonie a little mocking

126

bow. 'You must be Mrs Kramer. A real pleasure to meet you. And how lovely you are. Glen always did know how to pick his women. I hope you know who we are. It'll save a lot of explanations.'

Cameron let her go and saying, in a sulky voice, 'You're the Hayes gang,' the girl went over to Glen and he put an arm round her.

'A touching sight,' Hayes mocked and he bowed again. 'At your service, dear lady. And this,' he propelled Nita forward, 'is Nita. Now I doubt very much if Glen has told you about her. She's pretty too, ain't she? And once she was his favourite whore. Ain't that right, my darlin'?'

'It was a long time ago,' Nita said to Leonie who was looking at her with a shocked expression. 'Long before he met you.'

'What's she doing here? I don't want someone like her in my house.' Leonie's voice was shrill with shock and fear.

'Hush,' Glen said, stroking her hair.

'It's OK. Don't worry. Nita means us no harm.'

'Except mebbe to steal your husband away,' Cameron sniggered.

'Now, Mrs Kramer, we're all hungry after our long journey here. So why don't you go on into your kitchen and fix us somethin' to eat? I hope you're a good cook. Harve, go with her, make sure she don't get no stupid ideas about knives.'

'Go on.' Glen gave Leonie a gentle push. 'It'll be all right.' Of course they both knew he was lying, but Leonie tried to smile as she followed Murdoch out of the room.

Hayes pulled out a chair and slumped down at the table, indicating for Nita to sit by him and Cameron and Glen to go round its other side. He kept his gun in his lap, finger on the trigger as he stared at them all.

'Have to say, kid, ain't much of a place you've got here. Not for someone with fifty thousand stolen dollars in their pockets.'

'Thought you'd be living high off the hog somewhere with Nita,' Cameron added. 'Not grubbing about in the dirt.'

'Still, he has got a nice wife, so I suppose that makes up for a lot. I guess a whore like our Nita wasn't good enough for him, once he decided to leave the outlaw trail behind.'

'It wasn't like that.'

Nita said, 'Glen never loved me. But at least he was nice to me, not like the rest of you.'

'Does your little wife know about you and Nita?' Hayes asked.

'No.'

'Oh dear, then perhaps we'll have to tell her all those things you two used to get up to.'

'There's no need for that,' Nita protested. 'What good will it do?'

'It'd give me a helluva lot of satisfaction.'

'Now you've found me you can let Nita go.'

Apart from grinning at Cameron, Hayes took no notice of Glen, saying instead, 'Tell me about Antelope Wells.'

Rather taken aback at this sudden change of subject, Glen said, 'What's to tell? It's a nice town. A farming community mostly, with a few ranches roundabout.'

'A place with a lot of money?'

'No.'

Hayes laughed as if he didn't believe Glen and Glen wondered what the man was thinking and planning. He knew in that moment that Leonie had been right. Whatever the consequences to himself, he should have warned Max Sunderland that the gang was likely to come here.

A little while later, Leonie, helped by Murdoch, came in with stew, bread and coffee. It was obvious she'd been crying, but was making an effort to be brave for Glen's sake.

After she sat down she said, 'Mr Murdoch tells me you want the money you stole from the Tucson bank — '

'Yeah, our fifty thousand bucks,' Cameron said with his mouth full.

'Then we can be on our way.'

'I only wish we could give it to you. Haven't you told them, Glen?'

'Told us what?' Hayes asked sharply, looking at them both.

'I ain't got the money.'

'Well, son, you ain't spent it all on this place, that's for sure. I ain't stupid enough to believe that, so don't try lying to me.'

'I'm not lying. I sent the money back.'

For a moment there was silence, as the three outlaws looked at one another, at Glen, then at each other again. Finally Hayes burst out laughing, a laugh that slowly died away into an even deeper silence.

He said quietly, ominously, 'I don't believe you.'

'It's the truth.'

'Then why didn't Warden Bright tell us? He musta known.'

'I don't know.'

Cameron said, 'Mebbe the bastard was waiting for exactly the right time.

Or mebbe,' he shrugged, 'because it didn't affect him, he wasn't interested and so just didn't bother to say anythin'.'

'That's probably it,' Murdoch agreed. 'After all, we weren't meant to get out and have it to spend.'

Hayes suddenly banged a hand down on the table, making them all jump, and stood up so abruptly his chair fell out from under him. 'How can anyone be so goddamned stupid? Fifty thousand dollars! And you gave it back? You stupid bastard!' He pushed Glen, knocking him off his chair.

'It was the right thing to do,' Leonie said in a small voice.

'Oh, the right thing, really? Well, that's OK then! And I suppose it was you, you silly little bitch, who persuaded him to do it?'

'No, it wasn't,' Glen said, picking himself up from the floor. 'Leonie had nothing to do with it. It was my decision. I knew the difference between right and wrong myself. That money caused the deaths of two innocent men. It was tainted. I didn't want it.'

'You stupid bastard,' Hayes repeated. Then he smiled. A most horrible smile. 'Well, if that really is the case, we'll have to see what other money we can steal to make up for it, won't we? And, Glen, you'll help us again. And this time you're the one who'll run the risks of being caught. Perhaps even being shot and killed into the bargain.'

'I told you, I don't want anything to do with you or your robberies.'

Hayes smiled again. 'Oh, but my dear boy, I can make you see you ain't got no choice.'

14

It was much cooler in Flagstaff than down in the desert. The country all round was much greener too. Both came as a welcome relief.

When Judd reached the small town, he made a visit to the town marshal.

Marshal Ryan was in his forties, a capable lawman who had been keeping the peace in Flagstaff for several years.

He sat across his desk from Judd and said, 'Yeah, I remember all the fuss the Hayes gang caused down in Tucson. In fact, we had a few editorials in our paper about lawlessness in general, and how thankful we should all feel that the Hayes gang in particular had been caught; especially as they'd once robbed the bank here in town. What they got then was small potatoes compared with what they stole from Tucson, and luckily no one was hurt. There were more questions about why they weren't sent to the gallows. Our editor, if you ain't guessed, is firmly on the side of law and order.' Ryan smiled. "Course he's spitting nails now they've escaped!'

'I bet.'

'Must say it's a mystery how it was allowed to happen.'

Judd shrugged. 'It was a combination of circumstances. Nothing to do with Hayes. Although that's not to say he wouldn't eventually have found some means to escape.'

Ryan leant back in his seat, tipping the chair so it rested on two legs. 'And you say that another member of the gang got away at the time of the robbery and headed in this direction?'

'So I've been told.'

'Never heard nothing like that at the time.'

'Evidently he hadn't been with them long enough for anyone to learn his name.'

'But you know it now?'

'Yeah. It's Glen Kramer. Twentyish.

Good-looking, with light brown hair and blue eyes. Tall. Slim. Ring any bells?'

Judd had thought coming here was a long shot. That it was unlikely Ryan would remember one young man from two years ago, when numerous young men must pass through Flagstaff.

Therefore he was surprised when Ryan came down off his chair with a thump and said, 'Hell! Kramer! You don't say? Oh Christ!'

'What's the matter?' Judd asked, for Ryan suddenly looked very worried.

'He came here all right. And he married young Leonie Drury. It was the talk of the town.'

'Why's that?'

'Well, Leonie was a pretty girl, with a lively personality. Hard worker too. Coming up to nineteen. Practically every unattached male in Flagstaff and all around was after courting her. Then along comes this Glen Kramer. Outfoxes 'em all.'

'How did they meet?'

'It was here in town. In the café. Kramer was in there having dinner, when Leonie went in with her folks on one of their few journeys into town. It was meant to be one of them love at first sight things. Within, what, three or four months he'd met her, courted her and married her. Her pa weren't none too pleased, I can tell you that. He didn't want Leonie to marry him. Said he never knew what she saw in the boy, and that he had a bad feeling about him.'

'What did you think?'

'I didn't know the boy well. But from what I do remember when he first came through here, he did have a sullen look about him. Wild too.' Ryan paused. 'No, not wild exactly. More like he'd been wild, but something had happened to make him think again.'

'The trouble with the Hayes gang.'

Ryan nodded. 'I see that now. But, Mr Judd, the boy changed. Or rather I suppose Leonie changed him. Brought out the best in him. And despite her sweet nature, she also knew her own mind and made it clear what she wanted. So, although Will Drury thought she could do better for herself, in the end her parents bowed to her judgment and wishes and gave her their blessing.'

'When they got married did they stay around here?'

'No. They moved away. Almost at once. Said they wanted a place of their own, which given Will's reluctance about the marriage was probably a good thing.'

'Any idea where they went?'

'I ain't, no. But her folks will know. Leonie will have kept in touch with them. Will and Ellen Drury. They're farmers. Good folks. Got a place a few miles out of town on the road to Williams.'

★ ★ ★

Well-tended crops grew in the fields. The few milk cows were fat and sleek.

138

And the farmhouse was fairly large. The yard surrounding the house was clean and tidy.

As Judd rode up two large dogs came round the corner, barking and growling, making his horse back up and act skittish. The dogs were followed by a tall, thin man who yelled at them to shut up.

'Help you?'

'You Will Drury?'

'Yeah. Who wants to know?'

'I'm US Marshal Judd. I'd like to ask you some questions about your son-in-law.'

'Hell! He ain't in trouble is he? Leonie ain't hurt?' The man looked worried, thin hands clutching at one another, as if he'd always expected to hear Glen was in trouble.

'No, she's not, not as far as I know.'

'You'd better come in. My wife is out visiting at the moment, which is lucky if you're bringing bad news.'

Judd followed the man into the house and along a short passage, to a kitchen at the back where everything was neat as a pin, and shiny copper pots and pans hung from hooks on the walls.

Drury came to a halt and faced Judd, hands on hips. 'What's this about?'

'Do you know where Glen and your daughter are living now?'

'Why? What's wrong?'

Judd could see no alternative but to tell the man everything. It was only fair to warn Drury about the situation, and anyway, he wasn't going to tell Judd anything without knowing the reason for his visit.

By the time he'd finished, Drury had gone quite white, and he sank into the chair beside the table as if his legs would no longer support him.

'Oh God,' he groaned and raised anguished eyes to Judd.

'What is it?'

'A couple of days ago two young people came by. A man who said his name was Rob and a girl he called Nita. The girl had a black eye and several bruises, and Rob said she'd fallen from their buck-board. He was quite charming, smiling and laughing all the time. My wife and I believed him. Why shouldn't we? Especially as, although she didn't say much, Nita also smiled and nodded agreement.'

'What did they want?' Judd feared he already knew the answer.

'They said they were friends of Glen's from way back. They'd heard he'd gotten married and wondered where he was now, as they wanted to pay him a visit.'

'And you told him?'

Drury put his head in his hands and groaned again. 'We had no reason not to. No reason at all. They looked a nice couple. Ordinary. But,' he looked up again, 'they weren't ordinary at all were they?'

'I'm afraid not.'

'They were part of the Hayes gang?'

'The man was. The girl was forced to go along with them because she once knew Glen. That's how come

141

she had a black eye.'

'Christ, Mr Judd, I knew that Kramer kid was a bad 'un. I warned Leonie but she wouldn't take any notice of me, and now look what's happened. Jesus, if I could get my hands on him I'd kill him myself.'

'From all I've heard Glen wasn't really cut out to be an outlaw. When he joined the Hayes gang he soon realized his mistake. People can change, and I think Glen did.' Judd thought none of that would be of any comfort to the man.

'Look, they mean harm to Glen. They'd have no reason to hurt Leonie as well, would they?' What good would it do to tell the man the gang was a bunch of ruthless bastards, capable of doing anything to anyone?

So all Judd said was, 'Don't worry. I'll do my best to catch up with them. Stop 'em before they have a chance to hurt anyone. Now where do your daughter and son-in-law live?'

'Near a town called Antelope Wells.

It's a couple of days' ride from here . . . '

'I'll make it quicker than that if I can.'

Drury stood up, shaking Judd's hand. 'I wish you God speed, Marshal. Please help my little girl. Don't let harm come to her.'

As Judd went back outside to his horse, he wondered if, despite his best efforts, he was already too late.

And he wasted more time by going back into Flagstaff to send a telegraph to Antelope Wells warning the law there that the Hayes gang was on its way. Only to find that the line was down. Judd rode away not knowing if that was due to the weather, an accident, or Hayes cutting the line.

15

Max Sunderland sat alone in his office. Earlier in the week, he'd sent Arthur King out to visit the ranches up towards Flagstaff, to warn them about the break-out from Yuma. It was a precaution. No one expected the convicts to come this way.

Sunderland had debated going himself: it would be something to do, a change of scenery and the chance to meet and chat over news with other people. But the taxpayers of Antelope Wells expected to see their marshal around town, and his absence might be remembered come voting time. So he stayed put while King rode off, not expecting to be back for several days.

Sunderland yawned. It was so damn quiet. He wondered if the Hayes gang had been caught. No word had reached the town, the telegraph seemed to be out again, but that didn't mean they hadn't been. Stretching, he got to his feet and went over to the window, looking out on to that part of the plaza he could see.

Three horsemen were riding by. With a smile he recognized Glen Kramer. Good. The two men with him kept close to either side. Sunderland didn't recognize either one, and he thought they were probably travellers Glen had met along the way. They might have news.

Grabbing up his hat, Sunderland opened the door and stepped out onto the sidewalk.

★ ★ ★

It was with a heavy heart that Glen accompanied Hayes and Cameron into town. To be involved with them and their plans was the last thing he wanted. Especially here, where people believed him to be a decent family man. Yet what choice did he have when Leonie and

145

Nita were back at the farm, tied to chairs, and guarded by Harvey Murdoch? And their fate if Glen didn't co-operate, had been made only too clear.

He wore a gun by his side, but it was empty of bullets. Hayes was taking no chances. He'd told Glen that in any shoot-out he was to draw his gun and pretend to fire it. The one to get in the way of any stray bullets.

'And make sure you act like you mean it,' Hayes warned.

The previous evening, Glen had been forced to tell Hayes all about Antelope Wells and the places where the most money would be kept.

'I think it'd be best to rob the general store first, followed by the bank,' Hayes had decided. 'We might meet some resistance in the bank, and so not get the chance to rob the store. If this MacKenzie is like all the other store owners we've robbed he won't put up a fight.'

'Neither of them will have anything

146

like fifty thousand dollars,' Leonie protested. 'You'll be wasting your time.'

'That don't matter none.' All that mattered to Hayes was gaining revenge on Glen — hurting him for the hurt he had done to the gang.

Now, out of the corner of his eye, Glen saw Marshal Sunderland come out of his office. 'Please,' he thought, 'don't let Max see me. Don't let him try and talk to me.'

He feared that as soon as they saw a badge, both Hayes and Cameron would fire at the man wearing it. They wouldn't want to risk being caught and taken back to Yuma; in any case they hated the law and lawmen. And Max wouldn't be expecting any trouble, not from Glen's companions. He was relieved when he saw one of the town matrons stop Max and speak to him.

They came to a halt outside the store, dismounted and tied their horses to the rail. Glen's heart was beating fit to bust.

Hayes glanced over at him and said, 'No trying anythin' stupid, kid. Don't forget the safety of your two women, their lives, depends on your co-operation.'

'Wonder how they're gettin' on with Harve.' Cameron gave a cruel smirk. 'Seein' as how they're tied up and helpless an' all.'

'He'd better not hurt 'em, either one!' Glen said angrily, bunching his hands into fists, feeling worse because he also felt hopeless.

'Don't get het up, Rob's just teasing. C'mon. Let's get this started.'

Glen leading the way, the three men went into the store. Mr MacKenzie was behind the counter, his wife over by the far wall, re-arranging some blankets on a shelf, while several women gossiped in the corner by the door.

They all looked up as the men came in, and MacKenzie smiled in greeting.

'Hallo, Glen, didn't expect to see you in town for a while. What can I do for you? Got more vegetables for me to sell?'

Hayes shoved Glen forward and with

a dry mouth Glen said, 'It's not so much what you can do for me as what you can do for my friends here.'

'Oh?'

'They want your money.'

'Pardon me?' MacKenzie tried to smile, as if believing this was some sort of joke. He glanced across at his wife who looked as puzzled as he did. And his smile died when he realized Glen was serious and as he saw the hard faces and eyes of the two men with him, 'Oh my God.'

'Get on with it,' Hayes muttered. 'We ain't got all the time in the world.'

And Glen, scared that MacKenzie wouldn't act quickly enough for Hayes and would be shot, pulled out his empty gun and pointed it at the man. 'Your money, now!'

Mrs MacKenzie screeched in fright and dropped the two blankets she was holding, while the shocked gossips huddled together, wide eyed and open mouthed.

'Glen, what is this?' MacKenzie

demanded, startled and scared. 'How could you? What's wrong? We thought you were our friend.'

'Yeah, and now you know different, don't you?' Hayes smirked. 'Hurry it up, ol' man, or young Glen here might take it into his head to shoot you between the eyes.'

'He will too,' Cameron added. 'Quite a bad boy is our Glen.'

'Please, Mr MacKenzie, just do it!'

With trembling hands MacKenzie opened the till and began to pull out the money, laying it on the counter. There wasn't a great deal.

As if it was a fortune, Hayes scooped it up greedily, shoving it into his pockets, handing some to Cameron, who did the same.

'There you are,' he said, 'see how nice and easy all that was. No need for any shots to be fired or for anyone to get hurt. And that'll stay the same way so long as you all keep quiet while we make our getaway. But if'n you don't, we won't hesitate to shoot. Good morning sir, ladies. Pleasure to do business with you.'

As they backed towards the door, guns keeping everyone quiet, Glen breathed a sigh of relief. Everything was OK. As Hayes said, no one had been shot. All right, the MacKenzies believed he was a robber — and so would everyone else when they told their story — but hopefully when all this was over he'd get the chance to explain why he'd done it. Even if people couldn't forgive him, surely they would at least understand his reasons.

Of course, they still had the bank to rob, where something could easily go wrong — for as Hayes said, they were likely to meet more resistance there. But if the MacKenzies remained in their store for just a little while longer, they could rob the bank and be out of town before anyone realized what was happening.

The door opened and Max Sunderland came in.

'Hi there, Glen, thought it was you.

How . . . ' Sunderland stopped, suddenly aware of the tension in the air. Instinctively he knew something was wrong. He looked at the men with Glen. Christ! One wore an eyepatch! Ted Hayes! What was Glen doing with them? Their guns were already out and pointed! They were robbing the store!

Sunderland dived back for the cover of the door, grabbing for his own gun at the same time.

He never made it.

Yelling 'NO!', Glen tried to stop Hayes but Hayes shoved him away. And as Mrs MacKenzie screamed, both he and Cameron fired.

The sound of the shots was loud in the store. The two bullets struck Sunderland, and carried him back through the door and off the sidewalk. He landed unmoving on the ground.

* * *

Tears kept forming in Leonie's eyes and trickling down her cheeks. And it annoyed her, because she couldn't wipe them away. Which meant that awful man, Murdoch, knew she was crying.

She was tied, hands behind her back, feet together, to one of the kitchen chairs. Nita was similarly tied to the other. They were helpless while Murdoch roamed the small house. She had, on more than one occasion, heard something smashing to the floor and breaking.

Earlier she had tried to free herself of the ropes. It was useless. They were too well and too tightly knotted. Her struggles only made the knots all the tighter so that now the circulation was almost cut off to her hands. And she and Nita were placed just out of reach of one another, so they couldn't help each other.

Leonie had given up, her head sunk forward. There was nothing she could do. No escape.

And what was happening to Glen? Leonie prayed neither he nor any of the townsmen would come to any harm.

And she prayed that the people of Antelope Wells would understand that he didn't want to help Hayes rob them, but had no choice.

And what was going to happen to her? And Nita?

Before he left, Glen had repeatedly told her not to worry, that everything would be all right, he wouldn't let any harm come to her. But last night, when she was locked all alone in the bedroom and Glen was the one tied up in here, she had heard Hayes and Cameron ill-treating Nita. She had no doubt they might take it into their heads to use her in the same way — would consider it fun. And if they did, Glen wouldn't be able to stop them.

And supposing when they left here they made Glen go with them? He couldn't stop them doing that either. She might never see him again.

So many awful thoughts flooded into Leonie's mind, she began to sob.

'Don't cry. Don't give them the satisfaction.'

Leonie looked across at Nita who was watching her sympathetically. The girl had tired eyes and fresh bruises on her face. Leonie still felt uncomfortable and unhappy at having the girl — a prostitute — who had once meant so much to Glen, here in her house. But it would hardly do either of them any good if she behaved stupidly and refused to speak to her. Besides, she would wecome another woman to talk to.

'It's just so unfair.'

'I know. I'm sorry. Some of it was my fault. I should have lied to Ted.'

'No.' Leonie shook her head. 'You're not to blame. I'd have told him what he wanted if he'd hit me.'

'Thank you.'

'Nita, on your way here did they tell you what they were going to do?'

'They came to find Glen and the money and to have revenge on him. Now they know there's no money, all they'll care about is their revenge.'

'And they'll have that by destroying

Glen's reputation in town?'

'Yes. They'll make sure he's caught and put in prison.' Nita didn't add that that would be only a small part of their vengeance. The largest part would be making Glen lose all he loved: the farm — and Leonie. The girl could work that out for herself.

'But I can tell everyone Glen wasn't to blame . . . oh! They're going to kill us, aren't they?' Fresh tears came into Leonie's eyes, and she blinked them away.

'Probably. When we are of no more use to them.'

'And once they've done what they want, they'll head for Mexico, where they'll be safe from pursuit?'

'Yes.' Again Nita didn't say that the men might well take them along — to use — for part of the way. Leonie could work that out as well.

'Isn't there anything we can do?'

Nita shrugged. 'We can watch for any opportunity to escape or defeat them.' But she didn't sound very hopeful that

that opportunity would come along.

'Nita?'

'Yes?'

'Did you love Glen?'

'Yes.' A little smile passed across Nita's mouth as if all this was worth it for once having known the young man.

'And did he love you?' Leonie held her breath, waiting for the other girl's answer.

'A little, I think, but not in the way he loves you. And, Leonie, it was over for him a long time before he met you. You have nothing to fear from me.'

'I know that now.'

* * *

Judd rode the horse as fast as he dared. Rested only when it was absolutely necessary, keeping going well into the night, starting again before dawn. Had some water from his canteen for breakfast. He was as tired as the poor horse. But he didn't dare stop. The gang were far ahead of him.

God knew what mayhem they were wreaking upon the innocent civilians of Antelope Wells.

He didn't want them to escape him now — not after all this.

16

Confusion broke out on the usually peaceful streets of Antelope Wells. Shots and screams! The Marshal lying on the dusty ground! What was happening?

Amidst the horrified cries of Mrs MacKenzie and the other ladies in the store, Hayes and Cameron hustled Glen out on to the street. Behind them, MacKenzie grabbed up the rifle he kept below the counter.

Outside, the curious were already gathering, only to scatter as Hayes and Cameron rushed out of the store, yelling and firing in all directions.

'Get down!'

'Take cover!'

Panicked voices.

Glen just had time to glance down at Max Sunderland. His friend lay unmoving, and there seemed to be an awful lot of blood seeping through his jacket and into the ground all round him.

'Someone get the doctor!' a voice yelled.

From behind them, MacKenzie called out, 'Stop them! Stop them!'

'Get on the horse,' Hayes said propelling Glen towards the animals. 'Don't try nothing heroic. They'll shoot you the same as they will us.'

And Glen saw this was true, as MacKenzie stepped out on to the sidewalk and, aiming, began to fire, wildly and inaccurately. Several bullets smashed into the window of the café opposite, adding to the turmoil, as people ducked the flying glass. From somewhere by the side of the real estate office more guns joined in.

Best to run away, and hope to be allowed to live by Hayes and explain another day. Glen scrambled up onto the back of his horse, grabbing for the reins.

Next to him, Hayes paused to fire at MacKenzie, but he missed as the man ducked back into the store. Laughing, looking wild and exhilarated, Hayes shoved his gun back in its hoster and put a foot in the stirrup, swinging easily up onto the horse's back.

Cameron was already spurring away down the street, firing to either side as he went, keeping low over the back of his animal. With more gunfire all round them, Hayes and Glen galloped after him.

When they'd gone, the shooting died away and the dust settled down, an eerie quiet descended on the town. It was quickly broken as everyone came out of their hiding places and gathered before the store, exclaiming, asking questions, crying with shock.

The doctor had arrived at a run and was bent down over Sunderland.

MacKenzie stooped down by him and asked, 'How is he?' He could see for himself it wasn't good. The marshal was grey-faced and ominously still.

The doctor looked up. 'He's still alive, which is about all I can say right now. It'll be touch-and-go. The one good thing is he's young and strong. That might help him.' He stood up. 'Get him to my place.' Several men hastened forward to do his bidding. 'Does Betty Sunderland know?'

'No, she's not here.'

'Then someone ought to go and tell her. Bring her to me. She might need to know.' The doctor paused to look back at MacKenzie. 'What the hell was it all about? It looked like Glen Kramer with them.'

'It was,' MacKenzie said bleakly, his eyes full of pain. 'He pulled a gun on me.'

'Jesus! Why?'

'I don't think he wanted to do it,' Mrs MacKenzie said, but no one took any notice of her.

'He always seemed to be a decent young man,' the doctor went on. 'Settled down with a wife and building a good life for them both.'

'I wouldn't have believed it myself if I hadn't seen it with my own eyes. And, you know, I think the other two were

Ted Hayes and a member of his gang.'

Gasps of surprise went up from amongst those who heard this statement.

'Hell, no! What makes you say so?'

'Hayes has only got one eye, wears a patch. So did this bastard.'

'And Glen was with them?'

'He was leading them!'

Shaking his head, the doctor hurried away. It was up to other folks in town to deal with the robbers. His duty lay in trying to save Marshal Sunderland.

'I'll go with him,' Mrs MacKenzie said. 'Poor Betty might need my comfort. What are you going to do?'

'I'm not sure, but something must be done.'

Mrs MacKenzie nodded. 'Be careful.'

* * *

After some ten minutes fast riding, Hayes deemed it safe to stop so they could catch their breath. From the vantage point of a juniper-covered rise, he looked back along the trail. No pursuit. He hadn't expected any.

He took a drink from his canteen, then grinned. 'Looks like we're OK. For a time anyhow. Till the good citizens set up a posse. And without their marshal to lead 'em, that might take 'em some while.'

He and Cameron laughed. Shooting a lawman, even if he was only a town marshal, made them feel good.

'You bastards!' Glen said, breathless with the ride and from anger. 'You had no need to shoot Max.'

'Sure we did. He went for his gun, you saw that. It was him or us.'

'No it wasn't.'

'Hell, shut up! He was just a marshal, he asked for it. Course there might be an able deputy to lead 'em. Is there?'

Glen shook his head.

'Didn't think there would be.' Hayes didn't have a high opinion of deputy marshals.

'Ted, how much did we get?'

'Not as much as if we'd robbed the

bank as well. Which we could have done if it weren't for that interfering bastard. Hell, I wish I could shoot him all over again.'

'Admit it, Ted,' Glen jeered. 'You got nothing. Just a few dollars is all.'

'Enough to get us to Mexico?' Cameron asked.

'Yeah.'

'I doubt it.'

'We are goin' to Mexico now, ain't we?' Cameron sounded a bit anxious, as if he wasn't sure that Mexico was still what Hayes had in mind.

'Sure. I said we would, didn't I? But first we've got to ride back to the kid's farm. Collect Harve. Deal with matters there.'

'Will we have time for all we wanna do?'

'Sure, Rob.'

Glen's heart twisted over. What did Hayes mean? What could he mean except trouble for him and Leonie? And Nita.

Of course he'd feared all along that

the robberies in town wouldn't be the only part of Hayes's vengeance for what he saw as Glen's betrayal. That he'd have something far worse in mind. Before he had time to say anything, Hayes was spurring his horse on and Glen was forced along with him. He could only hope that in Antelope Wells the posse was ready to follow.

★   ★   ★

It wasn't. Nothing had yet happened, except for a lot of shouting and arguing. The womenfolk stood on the sidewalks, their men milled around in front of the store. They wanted to do something, intended to go after the robbers, make them pay for what they'd done. It wasn't cowardice that kept them from acting. It was not knowing quite what to do.

Trouble of this kind had never come to town before. A robbery in broad daylight, attempted murder — it was unheard of. And that time some

166

drunken cowboys broken one of their number out of jail, Marshal Sunderland had been there to organise a posse. Sworn men in as deputies, ordered supplies, led them out. But Marshal Sunderland wasn't there now. He lay in bed at the doctor's, dying perhaps ... while Betty looked on, holding her husband's hand as the doctor removed the bullets and bandaged the man up.

If only the deputy weren't out of town. Arthur King might be slow and stolid, but he was dependable. But he wasn't there. It was up to the citizens of Antelope Wells to act for themselves.

'The first thing to do,' Mackenzie said, having called yet again for silence, 'is to put someone in charge.'

'What about you?'

'Me? I don't know ... ' the man's voice trailed away.

'Who else is there?'

'We need horses. Supplies,' someone else decided.

'And rope to string the bastards up!'

'We'll have none of that,' MacKenzie said.

'Yeah we will,' the same man said. 'And the first one we string up is that deceitful bastard, Kramer!'

Several others called out and nodded their agreement, making it quite clear that, even if MacKenzie led the posse, he wasn't going to order any of the rest about.

MacKenzie sighed. This was going to be much more difficult than he could ever have believed. And it was all taking such a long time — far too long. The Hayes gang would get away if they didn't do something soon.

17

It was into this confusion that Judd rode, on his arrival at Antelope Wells. When he dismounted and people saw his US Marshal's badge, they quickly crowded round him. And to his question of 'What's happened?', everyone broke out talking at the same time. He caught words such as, 'Robbery', 'Young Kramer', 'Never would have thought it'.

'Hold on!' Judd yelled. 'Quiet! One at a time.' When the excited yelling seemed about to start up again, he said, 'No! You!' And he pointed at MacKenzie, the one man who appeared to know what he was doing. 'You, tell me what's going on.'

None of what he learned from the store-owner surprised Judd.

'Can you help us, mister?' MacKenzie asked when he'd finished his tale.

'You are here after Hayes, ain't you?'

'Yes. To both questions.' A general sigh of relief went up. 'Look, I'll need a fresh horse. Mine's been ridden pretty hard the last few days. Can you arrange that?'

'Yeah, no problem.'

'Good.'

'I'll also get one of the women to fix you something to eat and drink. You look as if you could do with it.'

'Thanks.' Judd acknowledged MacKenzie's kindness. 'Also get as many men together as want to be in the posse. Everyone else should go home. There's nothing for them to do here. Get the men a mount and a canteen of water each. Some food. Not much, because I don't suppose we'll be long. But they should all bring along thick coats and a blanket, in case we have to stay out all night.

'All right.'

'While you're doing that for me, I'm going to see how the marshal is.' Judd sounded angry. He didn't like lawmen being shot, especially when it wasn't even in the course of duty, but simply because they were lawmen. 'Where will I find him?'

'I'll take you,' a small boy offered.

'I won't be long. Everyone should be ready to leave as soon as I get back.'

'I'll see to it,' MacKenzie promised, relieved to have someone other than himself in charge.

The doctor's house was situated on the corner of the road leading to the church. It was surrounded by a white picket fence and flowerbeds.

The marshal lay in bed in the back room. His tearful wife sat by his side, holding his hand, although he was unconscious and he was unaware of her. Mrs MacKenzie bustled around making coffee for everyone.

Judd pulled the doctor to one side so Betty Sunderland wouldn't hear their conversation. 'How is he?'

The doctor shrugged. 'Luckily the bullets were easy to get out. And neither of them hit anything vital. I've cleaned the wounds. But he lost a lot of blood. I don't know. Betty is a sensible woman. She'll help me with the nursing. Are you going after the bastards?'

'Yeah. Right now.'

'MacKenzie said it was Ted Hayes. Was it?'

Judd nodded. 'Yeah.'

'You know, I was down in Tucson when they robbed that bank. They were bastards then, they're bastards now. Never expected them to come through here. No one did.'

'They had a reason for it.'

'Glen Kramer?'

'That's right. Don't think too badly of the boy. I doubt whether what happened was his fault. Or whether he wanted anything to do with it.'

'I saw the bastards ride out of Tucson that day. There were four of them. Although others swore it was only three. And some made out five or six. When Hayes and the other two were caught, although the money was still missing, it was thought the gang must have hidden it or dropped it somewhere along the way.'

'Didn't anyone think the fourth gang member had it?'

'Oh yes, but by then his trail was nowhere to be found. The marshal and the prosecutor asked the gang about his identity and where he might go, but none of them admitted his existence. So he was forgotten about. Then, what, about six months later, Wells Fargo delivered forty nine thousand, five hundred dollars to the bank.'

'What!' Judd looked startled. 'The money was returned?'

'All but five hundred dollars of it. Of course that raised the subject of the fourth man all over again. After all, who else could have sent it back? There was talk of trying to find him, about sending someone to talk to Hayes in Yuma. But it was a five minute wonder and nothing ever came of it.'

'Why not?'

'Well, it was Hayes who'd done the

shooting, he and the other two were safely in prison and the money was returned. What was the point?' The doctor paused. 'And, Marshal, now you're telling me the fourth gang member did exist and was Glen Kramer?'

'Yes.'

'Somehow knowing that doesn't give me the satisfaction I thought it would.'

★ ★ ★

'Here they come.' Harvey Murdoch came into the room and grinned at the two girls. 'All safe and sound.'

'Thank God,' Leonie whispered.

She and Nita listened as horses were ridden up to the kitchen door and a few minutes later Glen was pushed into the room, followed by Hayes and Cameron.

'Leonie, are you all right?' Glen asked, going over to his wife, 'Oh, Christ, Ted, look at her hands. They're badly swollen. Do they hurt?' Leonie nodded, trying not to cry. 'I'm untying her.'

Without waiting for Hayes's permission he strode over to the sink, picking up a knife.

'Careful,' Cameron warned, a hand straying towards his gun.

'Oh, shut up. I'm helping my wife and you're not going to stop me.' And Glen sliced through the ropes binding Leonie to the chair. He turned and did the same for Nita, who looked at him gratefully and stood up, rubbing her arms, going over to the window.

Leonie cried out in pain as feeling began to creep back into her hands and arms. Glen immediately knelt down in front of her, taking her hands in his own, rubbing them gently.

He couldn't remember feeling so angry in all his life; not even when his stepfather used to beat him for no reason except that he felt like it.

'Murdoch didn't hurt you, did he? I'll kill him if he did.'

'No. Nor Nita either. But we were

both so scared. And worried about you. You seemed to be gone such an awful long time.'

'I'm all right.'

'Are you sure?' Leonie cast a look over his shoulder, where Hayes and Cameron were talking urgently with Murdoch. All three men looked excited, but somehow worried as well. 'Something happened, didn't it?'

'We robbed Mr MacKenzie's store as planned. That was OK, except for the look on Mr MacKenzie's face when he thought I was really in on it. And then . . . oh God!' Glen paused, putting his head in his hands.

'What is it?' Cold fear clutched at Leonie's heart.

'Oh God, Leonie, they shot Max.'

'Oh no!'

'I think he's dead.'

'Oh, Glen, no.' Tears came into the girl's eyes. 'Oh poor Max. And Betty. Whatever will she do? And everyone will think you were a willing part of it.'

'That's how it was planned,' Glen

said bitterly. 'The only good thing is,' he stood up to face Hayes, 'the citizens will be forming a posse right now, and as they know where I live, and know I'd never leave you behind, they'll be heading here right off. And it won't take 'em long either.'

'Cocky sonofabitch!' Hayes snarled. He hit Glen so hard round the face that he fell to the floor, skidding backwards to land against the stove.

'Stop it, don't!' Ignoring the pain in her hands, Leonie got up and went over to Glen, hugging him.

'Think you know it all, don't you?' Hayes yelled. 'Well, we ain't goin' to be caught that easy. And we'll still have plenty of time to carry out our plans.'

Pushing Leonie away from him and scrambling up, Glen said, 'What do you mean?'

Hayes came up close to Glen and leered into his face, while Glen glared back at him, determined not to show how scared he was.

'Tell him what we're goin' to do,'

Cameron urged, with a wicked smile.

'We're all goin' to have our wicked way with Leonie . . . '

Glen glanced at his wife, who looked at Hayes with horror in her eyes, but no surprise.

' . . . while you watch, and afterwards we'll shoot her dead. I don't much like shooting women, but I'll enjoy it this time to get back at you. Come to think of it, we'll probably shoot Nita too, now she ain't no more use to us. And then you're comin' along for a ride. For a while anyhow. Till it looks like posse has nearly caught up, upon which we'll leave you behind to face their wrath alone.'

'They'll think you've gone mad,' Cameron added, enjoying himself. 'Killing your beloved wife an' all. Mebbe in some sorta quarrel you whore.'

'No one will believe it,' Leonie said, more bravely than she felt.

'Bet they will.'

'You hurt Leonie or Nita, I'll find

some way to kill you,' Glen said, making all three men laugh.

'Don't see quite how, ol' son,' Hayes mocked.

'Somehow I don't think you'll have the chance to carry out any part of your plan,' Nita suddenly said. She turned from looking out of the window. 'You won't want to either.'

'Why not?' Cameron said.

To everyone's surprise Nita had a smile on her face. 'You might need hostages.'

'What are you talking about?' Hayes demanded angrily.

'Simply, Ted, that the posse is already here!'

18

'What?' Hayes exclaimed. Pausing to point a finger at Nita and say, 'And wipe that grin off your face or I'll god-damned wipe it off for you,' he rushed for the window.

The girl shrugged and went to stand behind Glen and Leonie, who were looking at one another with hope in their eyes. 'It's true,' she told them.

Which Hayes could see for himself as he stared out of the window. There was movement down there in the fields: the odd glimpse of a figure or two.

'Hell!' he exclaimed, turning back to his two comrades, who watched him with anxious faces. 'How the hell did they get here that quick? With their marshal dead I was sure there'd be time to do all we wanted.' He was red with anger at his plans being thwarted.

'It can't have nothin' to do with that

damn lawman who was in the desert following us can it?' Cameron moved to his friend's side.

'Don't see how. That was days ago, and we left the bastard for dead.'

'What are we gonna do?' Murdoch asked.

'Not give up, that's for damn sure.'

While this talk was going on, Nita stood close to Glen and brushed his arm with her hand. For a moment Glen wondered what she wanted. Then he realized he still held the knife he'd used to free her and Leonie. No one was taking any notice of them; the others were too busy discussing their situation. Quickly he handed the knife to the girl, and she hid it in the pocket of her skirt.

'Oh well,' Hayes said turning back into the room. 'We've been in some pretty tight spots before. Always got out of 'em.'

'Except when you were caught and sentenced to prison in Yuma,' Glen said.

'That's it,' MacKenzie said when they arrived at the farm.

Judd spent a few moments looking at the house and the area surrounding it. He thought the gang must still be inside, because three lathered horses stood tethered outside the kitchen door. There was another door at the front. No porch. Four windows. Having been built at the top of the slope leading up from the river, the house was in a good position for those inside to defend.

But it was also in a good position for those besieging the farm: numerous places provided cover. And, if necessary, it would be reasonably easy to get close to the house without running the risk of being shot.

'All right,' he decided. 'Mr MacKenzie, you stay near me. The rest of you spread out all round the house. Keep down. Try not to be seen. Don't take any chances. And no shooting unless it's absolutely necessary, or unless you get one of the bastards clear in your sights. Remember, there are two innocent women in there — '

'Two?' MacKenzie echoed in surprise.

'Yeah, two, if I'm not badly mistaken. And remember, Glen isn't one of the bastards either, so try not to shoot him.'

'Are you sure about that?' someone else asked.

'Yeah.' Judd looked up at the sky. 'It'll be dark soon. I can see us having to stay out all night. If that happens divide up into groups of three, one to stay watch for two hours then wake the next man. That way you'll each get four hours sleep. Cold rations I'm afraid. OK?'

There were nods and murmurs of agreement. It might mean an uncomfortable night, but the men were determined not to let those responsible for bringing violence to Antelope Wells get away.

'What do you plan to do?' MacKenzie asked, as the men slid away to each side.

'I'm not sure yet. My main concern must be for the women. But equally I don't want Hayes and the others getting away. This is my best chance to recapture 'em, or kill 'em, and, quite frankly, Mr MacKenzie, I'm not too concerned which it is. They elude me here, they could get to Mexico and be free and clear. I don't want that to happen.'

'What did you mean about two women? And about Glen being innocent, when I saw for myself he pointed a gun at me and demanded my money?'

'I'll tell you when we're in position.' And, lying on his stomach, and keeping to the shelter of the rows of carefully tended vegetables, Judd wriggled nearer to the house.

★　★　★

'What the hell are they doin'?' Hayes demanded, pacing up and down the small kitchen, pausing each time he passed the window to look out of it. 'Why don't they do somethin'? Why are they just sitting out there?'

'Pull yourself together, Ted, lead us,' Cameron said.

'OK, OK.' Hayes took a deep breath and calmed down. It was up to him, as usual. 'All right. Pull the shutters across the windows. Bar the doors. Show the bastards we mean business.'

* * *

'Something's happening up there,' MacKenzie said, as he saw the kitchen window being shuttered.

'Looks like they're getting set to stay where they are. Fools! Don't they know we can wait 'em out?' But waiting wasn't something Judd was good at. Besides, he knew that the longer the wait, the more risk to the innocent people in the house. For

185

Hayes obviously didn't have much patience either. 'I'm going to see if I can talk to them,' he suddenly decided. 'At least see if they'll let the women go.'

'Is that a good idea?'

'Only if it works.' Judd holstered his gun and, his heart beating rapidly at the chance he was taking, he got to his feet. Standing hands well away from his sides, he yelled, 'Hey you, you in the cabin!'

★　★　★

'Lookee here,' Cameron called Hayes over to the window. 'It is that goddamned lawman. He wants to talk to us!'

'It can't be.'

'Yeah it is.'

'Well, he might have escaped us once, but he won't again.' And Hayes drew his revolver.

★　★　★

'Mr Hayes, you are surrounded. You can't go anywhere. You might as well give up. At least let Leonie and Nita go.' Judd got no further as a rapid volley of shots came from the kitchen window. 'Shit!' he swore, and just had time to drop down on the ground before bullets whined over his head.

'I guess that answers one question,' MacKenzie said. 'They ain't in the mood for talk.'

'And I guess it means a night spent out in the open.'

★ ★ ★

'That's shown 'em!' Hayes declared, holstering his gun and looking mighty pleased with himself.

'They won't give up,' Glen said.

'Mebbe not.'

Cameron stared out of the window before closing the shutter again. 'I don't reckon they'll do anythin' now it's gettin' dark. They'll stay put hoping to sweat us out. Won't be too comfortable for 'em.'

'While we're all standing about in here thinking how safe and comfortable we are, the bastards could be sneaking up on us,' Murdoch pointed out.

Hayes grinned. 'We'll be ready for 'em. They don't know who they're goin' up against. Harve, why don't you stay here in the kitchen? Leonie you stay with him, make us some coffee and somethin' to eat. And keep the coffee comin', help us stay awake.'

'Best do as he says,' Glen said to her, as Leonie clutched at his hand, unwilling to leave his side.

'And do I make coffee and food for my husband and Nita too? Or are you going to starve us?'

'Oh hell, yeah, I guess so. The rest of us'll go in the parlour. Leave the door open between us. Come on, you two, move it!' Hayes pushed Glen in the back and Glen, aware of Leonie's eyes following him, went through into the other room. 'And any trouble . . . well, you know what'll happen.'

'Better tie these two up,' Cameron said, pushing Glen and Nita down into chairs. 'We don't wanna be watching them as well.'

'Yeah but not Leonie, I'm keeping her close by my side.'

Glen jumped up from the chair. 'You hurt her and . . . '

'And what? You're helpless, kid, and I have the upper hand, don't forget that. Don't worry, I ain't goin' to hurt her, not at the moment anyway. She's insurance to make you behave yourself. Rob, you go into the bedroom, keep a look out from in there.'

Hayes wasn't unhappy at having to stay awake and alert all night; it gave him time to think and to come up with a new plan.

19

Everyone in the farmhouse — captors and captives alike — spent a sleepless night.

Hayes feared an attack under the cover of darkness, and he and the other two stood watch at the windows. While Cameron and Murdoch got more and more spooked at imagined movement as the minutes ticked by, Hayes spent the time plotting.

Leonie lay on the floor by the man, trying to get some rest. But it seemed that every time she drifted away into sleep, Hayes woke her up, kicking and cursing her, and forced her to make them all fresh coffee.

Worried about her, worried about himself and Nita as well, Glen found it impossible to sleep. He wanted to do something, but he didn't see what he could do tied tightly to the chair. He was frightened of what the morning would bring. Hayes was determined not to go back to Yuma. He would do anything to stop being caught again.

Glen had no idea who was out there, leading the posse, except it was some unknown lawman. His first priority would be to re-capture the Hayes gang. Would he even care about what happened to anyone else?

And, even if somehow he wasn't killed, what then? He'd be hauled off to jail for his part in the Tucson bank robbery; land up in Yuma himself.

And what about poor Max? Was he dying or dead? Glen sighed. How could everything go so completely wrong, so quickly?

★ ★ ★

Max Sunderland blinked open his eyes onto a dark, strange room. That he was lying in bed was about all he could tell. Where was he? His body seemed to ache all over. He moaned with the realization of how much he hurt. Instantly his wife, who was sleeping fitfully in the chair beside him, was awake, bending over him, wiping his hair out of his eyes.

'Hush, hush,' Betty said, trying not to cry, for she had feared Max would never wake up again.

'What's happened?'

'It's all right. Don't worry. I'm here. I won't leave you.'

Puzzled by all this, Sunderland searched his mind. Suddenly it all came back: MacKenzie's store, the men with guns robbing it. And Glen Kramer was with them! The shots. He was hit and was falling — he shuddered with the remembered pain — then nothing till now.

He said, 'God,' and tried to sit up.

'No, Max, lie down. Please. You must rest.'

'Those men! Who were they? They shot me.'

'It's all right.'

'I must stop them. Find out why.

God, Betty, it was Glen!'

'You can't do anything now. Wait till morning. Hear what the doctor says.'

'No, I must . . . ' But a wave of pain and tiredness swept over Sunderland, and he didn't resist as Betty pushed him down in the bed.

'Go back to sleep,' she urged gently. 'See how you are tomorrow.'

Sunderland tried to protest, to say he was marshal and it was his duty to chase down the robbers, but he found his eyes closing. And he could do nothing to prevent himself slipping into a deep sleep.

★ ★ ★

Cameron slurped down the remainder of the coffee, peered out of the window to make sure no one and nothing was moving out there, and went over to Hayes. 'What are we gonna do, Ted? Have you decided?'

'Come morning we can't stay here any longer.'

'Why not? I reckon we're safe enough. We've got food and water, and the bastards out there won't risk rushing us.'

'Mebbe. But they can wait us out.'

'So what? They're just townspeople.' Cameron was scornful. 'They can't outshoot us.' He conveniently forgot it was a bunch of determined townsmen who'd caught them after Tucson.

'But they might send for help from the law up in Flagstaff. And, if so, that won't be long getting here. We'll be trapped.'

Cameron thought about that and nodded agreement. 'OK, so how do we get away?'

'We've got hostages in the two women. We use them as shields, the bastards won't shoot at us for fear of hitting them. And we take them with us until we know we're safe. Into Mexico if necessary.'

'How long d'you reckon it'll take us to reach the border?'

Hayes didn't admit to not knowing.

'We ride fast without stopping, a couple of days mebbe.' He thought it would take a lot longer than that, but Rob was spooked enough as it was without learning he had a long ride to safety.

'What about the kid?'

Hayes cast a contemptuous look at the young man slumped in the chair. 'He's of no use to us. Be a pleasure to shoot him before we go.'

★ ★ ★

Although Nita had cut her wrists on the ropes binding them until they bled, she had at last managed to reach the knife in her pocket. With it she was slowly and carefully sawing through the knots. It wasn't easy. She was tied tightly and efficiently. The rope was thick and strong. And she didn't dare work with the knife all the time for fear of being seen. But slowly the rope was loosening: surely she would soon be free!

★ ★ ★

Outside, the members of the posse spent an uncomfortable, cold night on the hard ground, with no fire, nor even a cup of coffee, to help the hours go by.

Judd pulled his coat further round him and snatched a few moments of sleep here and there. He was worried about the morning — wondering what would happen. He wasn't worried about the posse. They were good men, determined to do what was right: they wouldn't let him down in a fight. But what would Hayes do?

He hoped that the gang had spent the night thinking over their situation and be more inclined to give up come morning, but somehow he doubted it. Judd didn't want the blood of innocent young women on his hands. He would have to act both quickly and carefully.

He rolled over on to his back, looking up at the sky. It was already lightening — a lessening of the grey — in the east. Dawn wasn't far away. It would soon be morning.

20

As the other members of the posse started to stir, Judd took a drink from his canteen and raised himself up to look at the house. Nothing had changed. The shutters were still pulled across the windows, the doors firmly closed. And the three horses remained tethered outside the kitchen door.

He thought they might pose a problem if Hayes decided to make a run for it. They were close to the house, easy for the men inside to reach, and they would be rested after their hard run the day before. On the other hand, they hadn't been watered or fed, and Hayes might not want to take a chance on any of the animals breaking down on him.

'Morning,' MacKenzie said from by his side. The man had bleary eyes as he sat up and stretched. 'God, but what I couldn't do with a cup of coffee!'

Judd thought for a moment. 'I don't see why we shouldn't have one. It'll do us all good. Keep morale up.'

'We'll need a fire . . . '

'Don't see as how that'll hurt. It's not as if the men inside the house don't know we're here. And if the fire is built down below the trees it won't give our position away.'

'Good idea,' MacKenzie agreed.

'Get a couple of men to start a fire. Once the coffee is ready we'll go for it in ones or twos.'

'All right.'

'And I think it would be a good idea if a fast rider went back into town to find out whether the telegraph has been repaired. If it has, he can send out messages to all the towns around here.'

'What, asking for help?'

'No.' Judd shook his head. 'By the time help gets here it'll be too late. Anyway there's enough of us to handle Hayes by ourselves. But if by some chance we can't, and they get away, then other lawmen should be warned that the gang is on the loose and might be headed their way.'

'I'll get onto it right away.'

But before MacKenzie had the chance to do anything, Judd clutched at his arm.

'Wait! Listen!'

And from the house came the sound of a girl's scream, followed by a shot. Judd and MacKenzie looked at one another — what was happening now?

'Look!' MacKenzie pointed at the house.

The kitchen door opened.

* * *

'They're on the move down there,' Murdoch said, putting his head round the parlour door.

'So are we!' Hayes declared, kicking Leonie. 'Come on, girl. Get up. Harve, are the horses still outside?'

'Yeah,' Murdoch nodded. 'No one's

dared make a run up to the house to get 'em.'

'Good. We can take them. They're already saddled and bridled and they'll be rested by now. Rob, fill our canteens with water, grab up whatever food can go in the saddlebags. I don't want us goin' hungry on the way into Mexico, but I don't want us stoppin' any more'n necessary. Then let's get outta here. And once we hit the saddle we ride fast.'

Leonie looked at Glen and Nita who were still tied to the chairs. 'Are you leaving us alone?' she asked Hayes in a small, frightened and not very hopeful voice.

Hayes laughed nastily. 'Hardly, darlin'. Your troubles ain't over yet. In fact, they could just be starting. You and Nita are comin' along with us as hostages.'

'No!' Leonie cried and went over to Glen, putting an arm round him.

'You leave her be!' Glen said.

Losing his temper, Hayes yelled, 'I

am gettin' almighty fed up with people who are in helpless positions tellin' me what I can and goddamned cannot do!' He kicked aside a chair so that it bashed against the far wall and splintered. 'You've caused me enough misery as it is! This is my plan, and no one is goin' to spoil it! Least of all you, you bastard!' And with a roar of fury, he hit Glen round the head as hard as he could, sending the boy sprawling.

Leonie cried out, but before she could do anything Hayes grabbed her arm in a painful grip. 'You're comin' with us, and there ain't one goddamn thing anyone can do about it.'

'You too,' Cameron said, winking at Nita, as he returned from the kitchen with some tins of tomatoes.

'What about Glen?' Leonie asked. Please, she thought, please let them leave him here for the posse to find. A jail sentence would be preferable to anything else these dreadful men might have in mind.

Her hopes were dashed.

'Oh, I'm goin' to shoot the silly bastard.' And Hayes drew his gun.

Leonie screamed. As Hayes fired she knocked his arm down so the bullet ploughed harmlessly into the floor.

In a towering rage, Hayes swore and backhanded her across the face. She fell near to Glen. And immediately rolled on top of him, so Hayes didn't have a clear shot, for she knew the man wouldn't want to shoot a valuable hostage.

While all this was happening, Nita sawed through the last of the knots binding her wrists to the chair, gritting her teeth against the pain. With the attention of Hayes and Cameron on Glen and Leonie, she reached down slicing through the rope binding her ankles. And in one swift movement, she jumped up and raced for the kitchen.

'Stop her!' Hayes yelled.

As Cameron went to go after her, Leonie stuck out a leg. With a curse

Cameron fell over, and the girl kicked him hard on the shin.

'Ouch! You bitch!' Cameron reached down to grab at his leg.

Looking very surprised, Murdoch turned as Nita came into the room. She reached the door as he grabbed her from behind and swung her round.

'No, you don't.'

'Yes, I do!' Nita brought up the knife she still held and plunged it into the man's chest.

With a cry he let her go, stumbling backwards, blood spurting out from the wound.

With shaking hands Nita began to pull at the bolts on the door. She got them undone just as Cameron ran after her. Desperately, she flung the door open and ran outside.

★ ★ ★

'Wait! Wait!' Judd yelled as he saw her. 'Hold your fire!'

The men watched as Nita ran as fast

203

as she could down the slope towards them. Cameron sent several shots after her and those nearest to him fired back, driving him indoors.

Nita reached safety and came to a halt, bending forward, gulping for breath, tears of relief in her eyes.

Followed by MacKenzie, Judd strode over to her. 'Nita?'

The girl nodded, still unable to speak, surprised he knew her name.

'What's going on up there? Is anyone hurt?'

'Murdoch . . . dead . . . Ted is leaving . . . he wanted . . . hostages.'

'All right, take your time.' MacKenzie frowned at Judd and passed the girl a canteen. 'You're safe now. Get your breath back.'

She took a drink, pushed her tangled hair away from her face. 'I'm OK.' She looked at Judd's badge. 'You're the lawman they talked about. Well, you'd better act quickly, mister, or Ted'll kill Glen and take Leonie with him, and . . .'

'Marshal!' A shout from one of the men interrupted her. 'Someone's coming out!'

And Judd looked up to see the kitchen door opening again.

21

Cursing, Cameron slammed the door shut, just as several bullets smashed into it. He turned back into the kitchen and stared, unable to believe his eyes, at Murdoch's body. The man lay on the floor, blood staining his shirt red. It was obvious he was dead.

Hayes dragged Leonie into the room. 'What the hell is goin' on?'

'The bitch stabbed Harve! She's killed him!'

'Oh hell.'

Leonie choked back a cry of horror at the sight of the body — all that blood — a dead man — in her kitchen.

Hayes was angry rather than upset. Since their escape from Yuma, Murdoch had soon got on his nerves, always whining on about something or the other. And when you followed the

206

owl-hoot trail, you took your chances. All the same, it didn't sit right that Murdoch had been killed, not during a robbery or a shoot-out, but stabbed by a girl, who was meant to be their prisoner! Even worse, the girl had escaped, and he could do nothing to punish her.

'She's probably down there right now telling that goddamn lawman all our plans.'

Cameron peered out of the window. He couldn't see anything. 'What shall we do?'

'It doesn't really change much,' Hayes decided. 'Instead of three of us and two hostages, there are two of us and we've just got the one hostage. They still won't shoot at us and risk killing this 'un.' He pulled at Leonie's hair, making her squeal in pain.

'What about the kid?'

'Oh, leave him. We ain't got time. We can always deal with him later.'

Cameron didn't ask how Hayes thought that would be possible. All he was worried about was getting away.

'Fetch the canteens and the saddlebags and let's go.' Hayes drew his gun and put an arm around Leonie's neck, pulling her close in front of him. 'And you, miss, are goin' to be our shield.'

Leonie didn't care about that. She actually felt happy. Glen was safe!

* * *

Everyone stood still watching as Hayes, with Leonie held tightly before him and Cameron close behind, stepped out of the house.

'No shooting,' Judd warned. There was no danger of that, as the posse members recognized Leonie. They didn't want to hurt her. He stepped forward so Hayes could see him.

'Hold it right there, lawman!' Ted yelled. 'We don't want no more trouble. And I'm sure you don't wanna see this little gal shot.'

'You know you can't get away with

this,' Judd called back. 'Why not give up?'

Hayes just laughed. And indeed there seemed little Judd could do as the men mounted two of the horses tied outside the door. Hayes kept Leonie by his side, pulling her into the saddle in front of him, so that at no time was there a clear enough target even for Judd, good shot though he was, to risk firing.

Cameron freed the third horse, holding on to its reins, intending to take it along.

'Don't try to follow us. That way, we get far enough away from here, we'll let the gal go, unharmed.'

'Don't believe him,' Nita said from close by Judd. 'They mean to kill her.'

'Don't worry, I wouldn't believe whatever Hayes said!'

The two men spurred away and were soon lost to sight over the far ridge. A little later came the sound of the horses splashing through the river, followed by silence.

'What now?' MacKenzie asked.

Judd came to a decision. 'We don't follow them, yet. Let them think they've beaten us. Hopefully that way Leonie will be safe for a while. Mr MacKenzie?'

'Yeah?'

'Get a man to ride into town to see about sending those telegraphs. And make sure he adds a warning about a hostage. Not that I intend to let them get very far.'

Nita plucked at Judd's sleeve. 'What about Glen? Are you going to see if he's all right?'

'Of course I am. First I want to make sure of all my options. Only two of the gang left the house — '

'Yes,' Nita interrupted impatiently. 'But it's all right, Murdoch is dead.'

'So you said. How do you know? What happened?'

'I stabbed him.'

Well, that sounded final enough. 'Are you certain he's dead?'

'I think he must be.'

'Would Hayes leave him if he was only wounded?'

Nita nodded, 'Probably. Especially if he'd slow them up. Ted's never been one for sentimentality. But, mister, even if Harvey's not dead, he's sure bad enough hurt he won't be any problem to you.'

'OK. We'll go on up. You stay here.'

Nita had no intention of doing that. And as Judd strode up the hill, one gun out and ready to fire, she followed amongst the others. Cautiously Judd used the barrel of his Colt to push open the door. He immediately saw Nita was right, and Harvey Murdoch wouldn't present any sort of threat ever again.

'Get the body out of here,' he ordered a couple of the men, and with the rest went through the door leading into the parlour.

'Glen!' Nita cried and pushed by them all to run over to the young man.

Helpless, tied to the chair, Glen still

lay on the floor where Hayes's punch had put him.

'Oh, thank God you're all right! They didn't shoot you.' Tears running down her face, Nita began to tug unsuccessfully at the ropes binding the boy.

'Here, let me,' MacKenzie pulled out a knife. As he helped Glen to his feet, he added, 'You've got some explaining to do, young man.'

'I know, I'm sorry,' Glen rubbed his arms and looked beyond the store-owner at Judd. 'Leonie?'

'They took her.'

'Oh no.' Glen groaned and sank down on to the chair MacKenzie had righted, while Nita put a comforting hand on his shoulder. 'They're going to kill her.'

'Not if I have anything to do with it.'

'It's all my fault.'

'It won't do any good to blame yourself.'

'You won't let them get away with this, will you?'

212

'No. I'm going after them.' Judd turned back to the rest of the posse. 'Alone.'

'Alone?' MacKenzie looked at Judd startled. 'You can't. It'll be too dangerous.'

'It'll be more dangerous for Leonie if we all chase after them. They'll see our dust for miles. I go by myself, they won't know I'm coming until I catch up.'

'I suppose that makes sense, but,' MacKenzie shook his head, 'I don't like it. You could be hurt, and no one would ever know.'

'I won't take any chances.'

'If you think it's best for Leonie . . . '

'I do.'

'All right. And you, young man, you're coming back to town with us. Answer a few questions.'

Glen stood up, an anguished look on his face.

'No, wait, wait. Please, sir,' he turned to Judd, 'please let me go with you. Please. It's my wife they've got with them. My wife they might hurt. I'll go crazy if I have to sit in jail and do nothing to help her. I promise I won't cause you any trouble. And I'll come back to Antelope Wells with you afterwards. Please.'

22

'Umm, I don't know,' Judd preferred acting alone, doing exactly as he wanted, without having to worry about anyone else. And Glen was an amateur, who would be difficult to control — who might be hurt.

'Please.'

Yet he had suffered quite enough, through little fault of his own, and so had Leonie, a completely innocent party in all of this, without Judd making either one suffer more.

He came to a reluctant decision. 'All right.'

'Oh, thank you, I won't forget this.' There were tears in Glen's eyes.

'Hey, now wait a minute,' MacKenzie said angrily. 'The boy helped rob my store. Our marshal was shot. He should be taken back to town so it can be sorted out.'

'Don't worry, Mr MacKenzie, I'll make sure he faces up to his responsibilities.'

MacKenzie could tell that no matter what he might say or do, it would make little difference now that Judd's mind was made up. And obviously things weren't as straightforward as they had once seemed.

'Well, I suppose Leonie's safe return is the most important thing . . . '

'I promise to explain everything to you,' Glen said. He paused, then went on, 'Do you know how Max is? He's not dead is he?'

MacKenzie shook his head. 'He was still alive when we left town, but we don't know if he is or not now.'

Judd said, 'Mr MacKenzie, will you take Nita back to town with you?'

'Of course. My wife will look after her.'

'And take Murdoch's body back as well?'

'And I'll arrange for it to be buried.'

'Good. We'd better get going.'

216

'Have some coffee, something to eat first. You both look as if you could do with it. And you don't know when you'll next get the chance.'

Judd nodded, seeing the sense in what MacKenzie said. 'We'll have to be quick. We don't want to let the bastards get too far ahead of us.' He followed the man into the kitchen.

Nita found herself alone with Glen. She caught hold of his hands. 'I hope everything turns out right for you and Leonie.'

'Oh, Nita,' Glen hugged her close for a moment. 'Will I see you again?'

'I don't suppose so.'

'What will you do?'

'Go back to the Dawsons I expect. I know they're not the best employers in the world, but they're not the worst either. At least I know what to expect with them.'

'I wish you didn't have to. You deserve something better for yourself.'

'I'll be all right,' Nita smiled. She would be gone by the time Glen got

217

back to town, for even if the worst happened and Leonie were killed, she knew now he would never want her. 'Leonie is so lucky.' And she pulled away so he wouldn't see the pain in her eyes.

★ ★ ★

Almost as soon as they crossed the river, Hayes realized there was to be no immediate pursuit. So they stopped, letting Leonie ride the third horse. They tied a rope round her feet and under the horse's belly and Cameron kept a careful hold of the reins, so the girl couldn't make any attempt to escape.

Now, with darkness fast approaching, she felt exhausted, her whole body aching as she slumped forward in the saddle. Not only was she not used to riding, usually taking any trips in the buckboard, but the men had set a fast pace through difficult terrain. They'd stopped only a couple of times, and then only for a few minutes. She was hungry and thirsty, and felt dirty.

She said nothing, knowing to complain or beg would do no good — Hayes was hardly likely to take any notice. And she didn't want to draw attention to herself, especially now. She wondered if the men would stop for the night and, despite how tired she felt, hoped not.

'There ain't no sign of 'em,' Cameron said, turning once again in his saddle to study their back trail.

'Did you really think there would be?'

Cameron grinned. 'No. Useless bastards. Bet that lawman is angry that they won't back him up. He won't come after us on his own, will he?'

'Even if he does, what can he do while we've got our little hostage here?' Hayes grinned at Leonie in a way that made her flesh crawl.

During the journey he'd made a number of jibes about how now they had Glen in custody, everyone would forget her. Leonie didn't really believe that. Glen wouldn't forget her. But then Glen was just that lawman's prisoner. And it might be that the lawman would prefer the bird he had in his hand rather than the two escaping into the bush.

'We'll go on for a while yet, till it gets dark anyway. There seem to be a number of good spots to rest up around here.' Despite Hayes's earlier intention to keep riding, he no longer thought that was necessary.

Cameron didn't remind him about it, because he knew what Hayes had in mind to do to the girl — and he wanted his own turn.

Seeing the two men look at her, then at one another and grin, Leonie shuddered. She began to pray for rescue, with no real hope her prayers would be answered.

* * *

'Mr Judd, what do you think Hayes will do?'

'About Leonie?'

'Yes.'

'Well, you know him better'n I do. If he's got any sense he'll keep her alive at least until he reaches Mexico. Even if he believes I've given up the chase, he must realize he'll have to pass close to other towns with their own lawmen. He might need a hostage.'

Glen bit his lip. 'I dunno. Hayes was smart, but not clever. And what happens when they do get to Mexico? They won't need her then.'

'Don't worry, we'll catch up long before the border. They can't keep up this pace for long, especially with the country being so hard on the horses.'

The two men had ridden steadily now for several hours. Not riding as fast as Hayes and Cameron, but not falling too far behind them either. The trail led away from the river and through the hills, twisting this way and that through the cypress pines, and across the valleys in between. In this remote country they saw no one else, although once they'd passed some branded cattle grazing on the side of a grassy slope.

This was the first conversation they'd had, for Glen was too worried to want to talk. He wanted to urge Judd on, but instinctively knew the marshal was good at his job and was doing his best, even if his priority was not the same as Glen's.

'Mr Judd, when we do find 'em can I have a gun? I'll give it back afterwards.'

'I don't want any unnecessary shooting,' Judd warned. 'If I can take Hayes and Cameron alive, I shall.' At the same time, if he did have to shoot them he wouldn't lose any sleep over it.

'Even after all they've done?'

'Yes.' Remembering the slaughtered family at the ranch, Judd added, 'There'll have to be another trial, and I don't think either one will escape the hangman again.'

'All right.'

'And I really won't have any trouble getting the gun back?'

'No, sir, you will not.'

Judd had no doubt he could handle Hayes and Cameron by himself. At the same time there was little point in taking unnecessary risks, and he just might be glad of Glen's help.

'Here,' he said and gave Glen the gun from his left-handed holster.

Before long the sun set. The way through the hills soon became pitch-black. Judd wondered whether they should stop until morning. He didn't want to, not knowing if Hayes would travel all night or not, and not wanting them to get further ahead. But there seemed little point in blundering along in the dark, not able to see the trail they were following, maybe giving Hayes more of an upper hand than he already had.

He was just about to suggest that they come to a halt when Glen said, 'Look, Mr Judd, up there.' And he pointed ahead.

Amongst the trees, Judd saw the faint glow of a small campfire.

'Do you think it's Hayes?'

'Let's go and see. If it is, he's providing us with a convenient beacon, if it's some cowboys they'll have hot coffee they can let us share. But, Glen, be careful, no hasty movements that might give our presence away. We want surprise on our side.'

'OK.'

Glen meant to keep his word. But halfway to the flickering light something happened to make him break it.

Suddenly in the silence a girl's terrified scream echoed through the night.

'Leonie!'

Before Judd could stop him, Glen dug his heels into his horse's sides, and it leapt forward. The boy urged it into a gallop, riding recklessly through the trees.

'Oh shit!' Judd muttered.

He had no choice but to follow. He only hoped neither horse stuck a foot in a gopher hole, and that neither rider was knocked to the ground by a low-hanging branch.

23

Leonie screamed again as Hayes pulled her down on the ground by the fire.

'Shut up! Who d'you think's goin' to hear you?' Impatiently Hayes tugged at her skirt.

'Leave me alone!' Leonie tried to push the man away. For a while she struggled, but she knew she would never be able to fight off Hayes, let alone him and Cameron both.

'What's that?' Cameron suddenly said.

'What the hell is what?'

'That.'

'Oh hell, just some animal loose in the brush.'

'I dunno — it's gettin' closer.' Cameron drew his gun, and went to the edge of the light cast by the campfire.

And almost at the same moment Glen rode his horse into the clearing.

Shocked, Cameron leapt away from the animal, landing on his back. Cursing, Hayes rolled off of Leonie. The girl quickly scrambled out of his grasp.

'You bastard!' Glen screamed and fired at Hayes, missing each time.

Cameron quickly recovered from his surprise. From the ground, he emptied his revolver in Glen's direction. One of the bullets caught the boy in the arm and, with a cry of pain, he grabbed at the wound. His frightened horse slithered sideways, and he tumbled out of the saddle.

Hayes jumped up, drawing his own gun. 'Got you now, you sonofabitch!' he yelled. He couldn't miss.

★ ★ ★

As he neared the fire, Judd peeled away, thinking it would hardly do any good for both of them to ride into the camp. He aimed for higher ground and found a place amongst some boulders. Jumping off his horse, and snatching up his rifle, he scrambled amongst them, reaching a good vantage point just as Hayes aimed at Glen.

Judd triggered off several quick rounds from the rifle, not hitting anything, but having the satisfaction of seeing Hayes jump back in surprise before he could shoot the boy. The man flung himself down on the ground behind the bushes that grew beyond the fire, while Cameron also squirmed his way to a safe hiding-place.

Glen lay where he had fallen, and Judd couldn't tell if he was badly hurt or just disorientated. He was relieved when Glen sat up, saw the danger he was in and rolled away to where the horses were tethered, crouching amongst their legs. Leonie knelt some way away, her face white in the darkness surrounding her. Judd hoped she had the sense to stay put and not risk being used as a hostage again.

'It's that goddamn lawman!' Hayes yelled across at Cameron.

'He's got us pinned down.'

'Yeah, he has, hasn't he?'

Hayes took in what was happening. The horses beyond the fire. A lawman who was a good shot out there. Little or no chance of escape. Fancy going out in a desolate spot like this with no one to know. It was hardly the way legends were made. Maybe a miracle would happen to let him and Rob get away, but Hayes had long since realized he wasn't the sort miracles happened to. Hell! Then he grinned, well, everyone had to go out some time or the other.

'You know, Rob, if there's one thing I want to do it's take that bastard kid with me.'

'Don't talk like that, as if you've already given up. We could still get out of this.'

'Don't be stupid. I reckon our time has come. Because, Rob, I ain't surrendering. Understand?'

'Yes,' Cameron said unhappily. He didn't want to go back to Yuma either — better be killed than that.

'We've had some good times together, ain't we?'

'Yeah.'

'Then, Rob, you couldn't ask for better'n that.'

* * *

'Glen, Glen, are you all right?' Leonie called anxiously. She came up in a crouch, trying to see what was happening.

Cameron saw her. His heart skipped a hopeful beat. Maybe Ted was wrong — if he could grab her, maybe they could still use her to get away. It was worth a chance. He fired again in Judd's direction and stood up.

Judd could see his intention. No way! Taking careful aim, he shot him.

Cameron looked most surprised as the bullet struck him in the chest. His legs going weak, he sank down into a sitting position.

'Ted,' he said quietly and died.

'Aw, hell, Rob,' Hayes moaned. He sighed and reared up, dashing for Glen, yelling with fury as he went, firing his gun.

A bullet from Glen's revolver stopped him halfway there. He fell to the ground.

Wearily, Judd got to his feet. By the time he'd collected his horse and reached the camp, Glen and Leonie were in one another's arms, both crying over the hurt suffered by the other.

'Are you all right, both of you?' he asked.

'Glen's shot.'

'Serve him right for disobeying every single order I gave him. It doesn't look too bad, he'll be all right once we get him to the — '

'Look out!' Leonie screamed.

Heart thumping, Judd swung round. Covered in blood, Hayes had stood up, gun out and pointing. Even as Judd was drawing his Colt, Hayes's gun spat flame. Judd felt a stinging sensation in his side, spinning him round. He was aware of Glen shoving Leonie to the ground and shouting 'No!'

Before Hayes could shoot again, Judd recovered and stood side by side with Glen. Together they fired.

The bullets seemed to lift Hayes up and fling him back down. He landed face down in the dirt and didn't move.

'Hell!' Quickly Judd went to find out if Hayes and Cameron were dead. They were.

'You're hurt,' Leonie said.

Judd looked down at his side and pulled his shirt free of his trousers. 'It's just a scratch. It serves me right for not doing what I should have done first thing and just taking it for granted they were dead.'

'They are, aren't they?' Leonie glanced again at the two bodies.

'Yes, it's over.' Judd held out his hand for his gun.

Glen gave it to him.

'We'll stay here tonight. Rest up. Have some food. Tomorrow I'll take the bodies back to town. And, Glen, you don't need to go with me.'

'What do you mean?'

'You're free to go.'

Glen and Leonie gaped disbelievingly at him.

'But, Mr Judd, aren't you arresting me?'

'I've learned your story along the way and I can see for myself you're not an outlaw any more. Probably never was much of a one either. You and Leonie deserve happiness together.' Judd was aware that his actions wouldn't be too highly thought of by his fellow US marshals, but who was there to know?

'Oh, Glen,' Leonie whispered.

But Glen said, 'No. I can't do it. Not even for you sweetheart.' As he held tight to Leonie's hand he refused to look at her disappointed face. 'I gave my word I'd go back to Antelope Wells and explain everything to Mr MacKenzie and the rest. And to see how Max is doing. Besides, I don't want to spend the rest of my life looking over my shoulder, wondering if I'm about to be arrested. That was what I was doing before and I didn't much like it. It's not fair on you either.'

'But, Glen — '

'No. You deserve a proper home and family, a settled life. Not always living with the fear we'll have to move on in the middle of the night, just because someone had recognized me. I'd rather go back, face up to things, take my chances. You will wait for me, won't you?'

'Of course I will.' Despite the unhappiness in her heart, Leonie smiled. 'It's the right thing to do. I'm very proud of you.'

★ ★ ★

Judd walked down to the livery stable, accompanied by Max Sunderland. Judd's side was bandaged up but the wound hardly hurt. However, the marshal was moving slowly and stiffly, clearly still in a lot of pain.

'The doc says I'll be back to normal in a couple of months,' he said. 'Able to use my gun arm.' Which was lucky or how could he have continued as a lawman?

'You know, I used to wish for some excitement around here, but now I ain't so sure. Perhaps a peaceful life is best.'

'Yes, maybe.' Judd couldn't see that himself.

'Where are you going now?'

'I'm riding back to Yuma. See Warden Bright, report on how it all turned out.'

'I wonder whether he'll be pleased or sorry that the three men are dead.'

'I doubt he'll shed any tears. Nor will I. I'd rather have brought them in to face up to their crimes, but I'm not sorry I killed them.'

'No.'

'Max, young Glen helped me you know. Things won't go too hard for him, will they?'

Sunderland smiled. 'I doubt it. Now

they know the whole story, most everyone round here is on his side. After all, there's more than one respectable man on the frontier with a shady past. Of course, he'll have to stay in jail until the judge arrives for his trial, but that won't take too long. And I think the judge can be persuaded to go easy on him.'

'Oh? How's that?'

'Well, you see, he's my father-in-law — and Betty always has been able to twist him around her little finger.'

'That's good.'

Judd mounted his horse and rode out of town. Perhaps on his way to Yuma he'd call in at the Dawsons, make sure Nita was all right. Perhaps renew his acquaintance with Daisy. The thought made him smile.

We do hope that you have enjoyed reading this large print book.

Did you know that all of our titles are available for purchase?

We publish a wide range of high quality large print books including:
Romances, Mysteries, Classics, General Fiction, Non Fiction and Westerns.

Special interest titles available in large print are:
The Little Oxford Dictionary Music Book, Song Book Hymn Book, Service Book

Also available from us courtesy of Oxford University Press:
Young Readers' Dictionary (large print edition) Young Readers' Thesaurus (large print edition)

For further information or a free brochure, please contact us at:
Ulverscroft Large Print Books Ltd., The Green, Bradgate Road, Anstey, Leicester, LE7 7FU, England. Tel: (00 44) 0116 236 4325 **Fax:** (00 44) 0116 234 0205

BRAZOS STATION

Clayton Nash

Caleb Brett liked his job as deputy sheriff and being betrothed to the sheriff's daughter, Rose. What he didn't like was the thought of the sheriff moving in with them once they were married. But capturing the infamous outlaw Gil Bannerman offered a way out because there was plenty of reward money. Then came Brett's big mistake — he lost Bannerman and was framed. Now everything he treasured was lost. Did he have a chance in hell of fighting his way back?

DEAD IS FOR EVER

Amy Sadler

After rescuing Hope Bennett from the clutches of two trailbums, Sam Carver made a serious mistake. He killed one of the outlaws, and reckoned on collecting the bounty on Lew Daggett. But catching Sam off-guard, Daggett made off with the girl, leaving Sam for dead. However, he was only grazed and once he came to, he set out in search of Hope. When he eventually found her, he was forced into a dramatic showdown with his life on the line.

SMOKING STAR

B. J. Holmes

In the one-horse town of Medicine Bluff two men were dead. Sheriff Jack Starr didn't need the badge on his chest to spur him into tracking the killer. He had his own reason for seeking justice, a reason no-one knew. It drove him to take a journey into the past where he was to discover something else that was to add even greater urgency to the situation — to stop Montana's rivers running red with blood.

THE WIND WAGON

Troy Howard

Sheriff Al Corning was as tough as they came and with his four seasoned deputies he kept the peace in Laramie — at least until the squatters came. To fend off starvation, the settlers took some cattle off the cowmen, including Jonas Lefler. A hard, unforgiving man, Lefler retaliated with lynchings. Things got worse when one of the squatters revealed he was a former Texas lawman — and no mean shooter. Could Sheriff Corning prevent further bloodshed?

CABEL

Paul K. McAfee

Josh Cabel returned home from the Civil War to find his family all murdered by rioting members of Quantrill's band. The hunt for the killers led Josh to Colorado City where, after months of searching, he finally settled down to work on a ranch nearby. He saved the life of an Indian, who led him to a cache of weapons waiting for Sitting Bull's attack on the Whites. His involvement threw Cabel into grave danger. When the final confrontation came, who had the fastest — and deadlier — draw?